THE VILLAGE AT THE EDGE
OF THE WORLD

THE VILLAGE AT THE EDGE OF THE WORLD

STUART FRYD

Greenwich Exchange
London

Greenwich Exchange, London

First published in Great Britain in 2018
All rights reserved

Printed and bound by imprintdigital.com
Cover design: December Publications
Tel: 07951511275

Greenwich Exchange Website: www.greenex.co.uk

Cataloguing in Publication Data is available from the British Library

ISBN: 978-1-910996-19-5

to all those children who prefer
their stories a little bit darker

'The oldest and strongest emotion of mankind is fear, and the oldest and strongest kind of fear is fear of the unknown.'
H.P. Lovecraft, *Supernatural Horror in Literature*

1

The Village

ALEXANDER HAD LEFT HOME – THE HOTEL that he had been living in for the last three months – knowing that this mission with the Professor might well be his last. Now, lurching from side to side, the carriage's large wooden wheels seemed to find every dip and hole in the rutted track. Their journey from the town of Cardiby had been pleasant for the most part – smooth roads and blue skies. Villages on their journey had been warm and welcoming to them, perhaps thinking that they were father and son, happy to offer the two travellers lodging and food, at least until Alexander accidently mentioned their destination – the village of Bleakhope. Smiles that initially greeted them suddenly turned to tight-lipped grimaces when Alexander let slip where their business led them. The warm, sparkling eyes of tavern owners shrank to suspicious slits and friendly nods and raised glasses to toast their health were replaced with stony silences, cold looks and women who hastily ushered their children away. But since their task had pulled them north, the hospitality was not the only thing to have turned cold. Just a day before,

Alexander had worried that his pale, freckled skin would burn under a bright summer sun untouched by even the smallest cloud. Now it was as if this part of England had decided to skip the end of summer and the whole of autumn altogether and go straight to an early winter. A blanket of unseasonal grey covered the sky and patches of mist drifted over the moors. To compound the situation, the smooth main routes had turned into potted dirt tracks and it had slowed their progress to a crawl as their two horses struggled to find safe footing.

'Ow!' Alexander said, rubbing his elbow as the cart jolted again, banging him against one of the Professor's large, wooden cases.

'Not much further now. An hour or so I would guess,' the Professor said, not taking his eyes from the track.

Alexander knew it wasn't a guess. Professor Cordite never guessed. He meticulously calculated possibilities and made well informed hypothesses, but he never guessed.

As they swayed and bumped onwards, Alexander wiped the water away from his freckled face and off his mousy brown hair that flopped above his eyes. It had begun to rain. Not real rain. Real rain fell from the sky as drops. This was English rain – drizzle – the almost imperceptible kind of rain that hung and blew in the air, soaking you through to your bones. Alexander had packed and dressed for summer and was feeling woefully unprepared.

Professor Cordite pulled the leather collar of his full-length black coat high around his neck and dipped his brown, leather tricorn hat in front of his eyes, trying to keep the water from his grizzled face. He looked more like a highwayman than a university Professor to Alexander.

'I told you to dress for winter,' he said, as if he could read Alexander's mind. 'Did you at least remember to pack the crystals?'

'Yes,' Alexander answered confidently, trying to remember if he had in fact packed them.

'And you have your violin?'

'Yes,' Alexander answered, unsure why he would need his violin on such a mission.

'Good,' the Professor said, nodding to himself. They rode on for a while longer, the farms and villages left far behind, the land becoming ragged and rocky with wild heather adding some muted colour to the bleak, grey countryside. 'Damn, I didn't pack the iron bolts!'

'I packed them. And the silver crossbow bolts. Just in case,' Alexander added proudly. The Professor turned and gave Alexander a tiny nod and an almost imperceptible smile.

'Good lad. Your father would have been proud.' This compliment warmed Alexander more than any winter coat would have. At least for a while.

The roads and the weather continued to worsen the further north they travelled. The patches of mist had banded together and were now merging into a thick fog. Goose flesh appeared on Alexander's arms and he hugged himself tighter, although he wasn't entirely sure it was just because of the cold. An uneasy feeling had begun to grow deep within his stomach. The feeling slithered up his spine and he shivered, the hairs on the back of his neck standing up like the hackles on a startled cat. The horizon had long since disappeared behind a thick veil of grey and with each minute his world seemed to shrink. For a while before the mist consumed them completely, he could see partway across the moors. Strange standing stones stood like huge, solemn sentries watching over the few leafless and skeletal trees that had managed to find enough good earth to take root in. The putrid smelling fog grew thicker still and even the edges of the road were not clear in some parts.

'This is too dangerous. We should stop,' the Professor said. 'If the road turns sharply we could go crashing down into a ditch.' But Professor Cordite didn't stop. Alexander guessed that, like himself, the Professor carried that growing fear inside him too and didn't want to hang around longer than he had to.

The horses were walking so slowly they had almost come to a stop. Every step into the wall of mist took an agonisingly long time as the horses paused to survey their footing. The Professor looked around him – eyes darting to every shadow that moved in the mist. The horses grew increasingly skittish, snuffling and whinnying, taking bad steps and jerking the cart around. With growing dread Alexander wondered what could be scaring the horses that had been so placid until now, and realised that he had not seen another animal for some miles. Rabbits, deer, pheasants and sparrows, so abundant back near the last village, were now nowhere to be seen or heard. In fact, apart from the panting of the horses, the clopping of hooves and wheels of their cart, their world was silent.

As if in mockery of these thoughts, a loud cawing burst out from the back of the cart. Alexander jumped and spun around. A black crow the size of a house cat was sitting on the back of the cart staring at the Professor and Alexander, tilting its head to one side then the other. The Professor looked panicked at the sight of it but he tore his eyes away knowing that to lose concentration now as he tried to guide the horses down the last few miles of the lane could be fatal.

'Shoo, get out of here,' Alexander said, waving the bird away with his hands. The crow didn't flinch and cawed again, raising its head to the sky.

'Caw! Caw! Caw!' it taunted.

His heart now racing, Alexander tried to flick at the bird, desperate for the creature to fly off and leave them alone. It pecked out at Alexander's hand in protest, its glassy eyes cold and calculating and then flew off, disappearing into the grey, its raspy cawing echoing off the mist, making it sound as if crows were all around them.

'Whatever happens, don't run off. Stay with me and the cart,' Professor Cordite said, not making Alexander feel any better about their situation. Why would he run off?

The Professor stared behind them for a moment and then spun back around, whipping the reins.

'Ya! Ya!' he shouted, the horses springing into a blind canter.

Alexander turned and looked behind the cart to see what had terrified the Professor so much. Tall silhouettes of men loomed in the mist behind the cart. The horses broke into a gallop, lurching the cart into the air. Grabbing the side of the carriage, Alexander held on as they bucked and twisted this way and that, nearly throwing him from his seat. Finding the courage, Alexander looked behind him again and saw the silhouettes were still there. Somehow they were effortlessly keeping pace with the cart even though they didn't seem to be running or even moving at all. It was as if they were gliding upright towards them, totally unaffected by the uneven road.

'There's the inn, up ahead. Hold on!' the Professor cried out.

Although the building was still hidden by the fog, Alexander could see orange lights coming from windows some distance down the road. Gripping on as tightly as he could, he pushed his feet into the corners of the footwell, trying desperately to wedge himself in. A silhouette appeared in front of them and it seemed suddenly to Alexander that these were not shadows of men at all. The shadows' arms were too long, their heads too thin. The shadow that blocked their way in the thick mist ahead terrified the horses as much as it did Alexander. It sent the two mares careering off the road, their eyes bulging and desperate. They neighed and bucked, trying to shake off the cart, foam flying from their mouths. Alexander was shaken like a rag doll, smashing wildly from side to side as the cart snapped and cracked. There was an almighty splash as the horses led the doomed cart hurtling into a pond. Alexander's grip was broken as the cart was thrown onto its side and he plunged headfirst into the water, one of the wooden chests striking his head as he fell. Blackness engulfed him and he sank without a struggle to the bottom of the pond.

Seconds or maybe even minutes later – Alexander would never know how long he was under the water for – the Professor grabbed hold of the back of his shirt and yanked him up. Brown water exploded from Alexander's pale lips and he heaved in great lungfuls of air. His body fought with itself, wanting to breathe, be sick, and cough up the gunk that sat in his lungs all at once. There was an almighty pain from the side of his head and his eyes stung. Looking about himself stupidly, his head swimming and spinning, he thought he might black out. He surveyed the scene around him as if in a dream where he was merely a helpless onlooker. The Professor was trying to keep hold of one of the horses, but it rose up and tore the reins from his hands, turning and scrambling out of the pond to disappear into the fog. The Professor was now facing Alexander and shouting at him. He was shouting and yet it sounded so quiet. The whole world seemed soundless. Alexander tried to focus on the Professor's lips.

'Run!' he seemed to mouth. 'Run!' And the dream was suddenly broken and the world exploded around him with sound and clarity. The terrible whines of the horses as they disappeared off into the mist, the ghostly, shrill screams coming from all around the pond and the Professor yelling at him as he tried to free a case from the sinking cart. 'Run, Alex!'

Alexander tried to run towards the glowing yellow lights of the tavern, an oasis in the sea of mist, but the bottom of the pond was thick with silt and every step was a slippery effort. From both sides of the pond, the grotesque shadows appeared again, gliding towards Alexander, their impossibly long, dark arms stretching out towards him. He slipped, falling to his knees and swallowed another mouthful of gritty water. He spat and spluttered, turning to face his dark pursuers who were only a few feet away, their spiny fingers of shadow stretching towards his neck. Rolling fully onto his back to face them, he could do nothing to escape now. His eyes closed reflexively, his soaking arms shielding his face.

A blinding light in the dark burnt through the mist. Even with his eyes squeezed tightly shut he could see the light. An angel, Alexander thought. An angel here to save him.

'Get up!' a familiar voice boomed. The Professor, brilliantly lit, stood above him, a sulphur lamp burning impossibly bright in his hand. 'Run! Run and don't look back!'

Alexander did not have to be told again. He waded through the pond, scrambled up the bank and sprinted onto the dirt track, tearing headlong towards the lights.

The mist seemed to be closing in on him, dark shadows crawling from the corners of his vision. His pondwater-filled lungs burned and he thought his heart might give out, but he never slowed, not until the tavern seemed to jump out of the fog in front of him and he crashed into a large oak door. With its whitewashed walls and bright fires within, the tavern seemed to ward off the mist. Alexander allowed himself to look back, hoping to see the Professor behind him, but he was nowhere to be seen. He leant back against the tavern door, reassuring in its solidness, and tried to catch his breath. The oak door opened behind him and Alexander staggered, then tumbled back into a heap on a stone tiled floor. Blinding light from lamps around the walls filled his vision and he squinted up, feeling his head swim in the sudden heat of the tavern. Figures loomed over him and his vision slowly shrank to a pinhole.

2

The Tavern

VOICES. FROM SOMEWHERE FAR AWAY, ALEXANDER
could hear voices. He struggled to open his eyes and shake away
the grogginess. He sat up, feeling stiff and bruised and registered
a faint light coming through thin, tatty curtains that danced
gently in a draft at the end of the bed he found himself in. He
was in a small room. There were two other empty beds and a
small table in one corner that had the melted remains of a candle
on it. Dreams, because they must have been dreams and not
memories, of his journey began to creep from the shadows of his
mind. He swung his legs over the edge of the bed and stood up
feeling every muscle in his body shout out in protest. Dark yellow
and blue bruises covered his arms and legs and he had one
screamer of a headache. He reached up to rub at his temples and
felt a lump the size of a small egg. He vaguely remembered a
trunk smacking into him before he hit the pond. His heart began
to race again as the realisation that the horrors of their journey
had been all too real.

Someone had taken most of his clothes off and hung them in

front of the fire, which had burned down to dim embers in the hearth. He wondered if it had been the Professor that had helped him, and dried his clothes, and then he began to panic. He had no idea if the Professor had even survived. Limping to the window, he threw back the stained curtains and looked out. It was impossible to tell what time of day it was because the grey mist still hung in the air. It could have been early morning, midday or late evening – Alexander had no idea. The sun could not be seen behind the slate grey clouds. There was no sign of their cart or horses below and no one seemed to be around outside. The track past the tavern stretched off until it was bleached to the same grey as the mist and was lost from sight.

From the window he could just about make out the dark shapes of trees, shed of their leaves and looking damp and weary. The grass was a muted yellow, as if the colour had been drained by the mist. In the distance, about a quarter of a mile away, were the faint, dark shapes of a village. Bleakhope, Alexander guessed. This was the village they had set out to save. The end of their journey. Their final destination. A pool of fog covered most of the village, but the tops of odd houses, a church spire and a tower rose above the grey sea and, higher up on the hill, just the faintest of grey silhouettes against a grey background, was the manor house. What unsettled Alexander more than any of these featureless shadows was the stillness. Nothing moved. There were no lights on in the village, no animals moved, barely a gust of wind. There seemed to be no life at all. The world outside looked like a sepia photograph: frozen, lifeless and almost monochrome. But that wasn't quite true, Alexander noticed after a moment.

In one of the manor house windows, a faint light flickered, then went out.

He pulled on his clothes, which had dried out nicely, and went to the bedroom door. For a horrible moment he was convinced that he would try the door and it would be locked, but it opened easily and he wondered why he would have thought such a strange thing. Outside was a narrow corridor which, Alexander found out as he began to walk around, had been made by only using the noisiest floorboards possible. Murmuring and talking below began to die down as he squeaked his way to the top of the staircase. The near silence that suddenly fell on everyone was louder than if everyone had been singing. Even the whispers stopped as he made his way down the wooden stairs and all faces turned to look. Men, women and children, all huddled around tables or gathered at the tavern bar, stood still and stared. The tavern was made from thick, black timbers and white plaster that had stained a dirty yellow from clouds of pipe smoke. The whole building slanted at odd angles with walls that were far taller at one end than the other. The villagers looked downtrodden, weary and haggard – like at the end of a very long wake after a funeral. Their clothes were simple, creased and dirty. Bags hung under their eyes, as if none of them had properly slept for a very long time.

The aching in his head flared up again and he gave his audience a pained nod. 'Good day,' he said. No one responded. They didn't even look uncomfortable just staring at him in silence, as if they were watching a particularly sombre scene being acted out from a play.

'I travelled with an older man. I would very much like to know if he is safe. Did he manage to make it here?'

An elderly man, who was balding on top but had mad, wispy hair flying about his ears and a wild, white beard, made his way towards him. He wore a fur-trimmed black coat and baggy, brown trousers.

'Welcome to the village of Bleakhope, young man,' the gentleman said and held out his hand for Alexander to shake. 'The Professor is fine. I'm sure it'll take more than a few shadows and a dip in our pond to keep him down if the stories about him are true.'

'Alexander. Pleased to meet you,' Alexander managed to say, and shook the man's hand. It was a rough, firm handshake that took Alexander by surprise. It was a far stronger grip than his balding grey head suggested he would be able to muster.

'The name's Mr Peter Parnell, and I have the ill fortune of being this damned tavern's landlord. I'm not blaspheming when I say that either, boy. I won't have blasphemy in my inn. The village of Bleakhope is truly damned. We have been forsaken and the village left for goodness knows what devilry. I'm thankful the Professor answered our pleas, but why he'd bring a young lad like you into this mess I don't know,' Mr Parnell said looking around at everyone in the tavern, still all watching in silence. 'You took quite a knock to the head, my boy. You alright?'

'I think so,' Alexander said, rubbing his temple again and running his fingers over the bump. 'Is the Professor here?'

Right on cue, Professor Cordite burst through the giant oak front door and everyone jumped.

'Alex, you are alive. Good,' he said with no hint of a smile. 'Help me with this case. I managed to drag it from the pond,' he said, dropping the large chest to the ground with a squelching thud. 'Go through it and see what materials we have lost and what can be saved.'

'For goodness sake, Professor Cordite. The boy has just woken up. Let him eat some breakfast first and get something to drink,' the landlord said.

Alexander had been about to do exactly as the Professor had asked – there had been no thought of refusing. The Professor seemed to think about Mr Parnell's request for a moment, rubbing his stubble-covered chin, and then shook his head – not in refusal, but as if to shake some sense into himself.

'You are quite right,' he said with a nod. 'Eat quickly, then give me a hand.'

Alexander nodded, secretly relieved. He suddenly realised how hungry he was. Holding his rumbling belly, he looked around for somewhere to sit. Free spaces seemed to magically disappear as bottoms shuffled closer together whenever he took a step towards them. He had got used to not being welcome in the towns they had passed through, but the villagers assembled in this tavern in Bleakhope were taking passive hostility to a brand new level. Alexander felt as welcome as a terrier at a rat's picnic, but he said nothing and felt the heat of his swallowed emotions begin to turn his pale cheeks red. The Professor had warned him to expect a reaction like this, but it was still hard to take. They were there to help. The villagers had written to them, why were they being so cold?

In the end a bearded, ruddy-faced man dressed in a simple greying shirt and grey woollen tunic made some room for him at a bench at the bar. He sat over a bowl of food as if he were guarding it. Alexander was not sure how much of the food the man had actually eaten as most of the meal seemed to have been caught in his beard and moustache.

'Sit here, boy. Don't mind us folk. If you'd seen half the things we have, you wouldn't trust strangers either,' the man said, with a mouth full.

'Thank you. The name's Alexander,' he said, holding out his hand. The man simply looked at it, nodded and continued eating his breakfast which consisted almost entirely of sausages.

'Lord knows what you and that charlatan are going to do when you see what's really out there. Have an accident in your trousers and run all the way home, I suspect,' the man said, staring ahead at nothing in particular then back to his breakfast. 'I'm Arty by the way.'

'Pleased to meet you, Arty,' Alexander said, not at all sure that he was pleased to meet him in the slightest. 'The Professor is a great man. He is very well known in India and London. There was a library in the town of Burntwood that was haunted by three ghosts and the Profess – '

'Maybe he's got you fooled as easily as Mr Parnell. Or maybe you're in on his little act. Either way, you're wasting your breath on me, boy. Whatever conjuring tricks he hopes to impress us with, it won't work on us, and it sure as heck won't work on those things out there,' he said, pointing a sausage towards the gloom outside.

A tin plate with a boiled egg, a rasher of crispy bacon and a small roll were placed in front of Alexander, and the barman walked off without saying a word.

'I saw the shadows as I came in. They chased me to the doors of this tavern,' Alexander said, keen to earn some recognition for his experience.

'Shadows? Pah! They're nothing! We let the children play with them,' Arty snorted, and Alexander knew he was being made fun of.

'Well, what have *you* seen?' Alexander asked, leaning in conspiratorially. Arty looked around him, wiping his greasy lips with the sleeve of his stained shirt.

'There are things I've seen that would make a boy like you go mad. Things that would make you scream out for your mummy and make you wish you'd never come to Bleakhope.'

'Like what?' Alexander asked, and Arty's face began to darken as he swallowed back a lump in his throat and his hand, clutching a fork with the last of his sausage on, began to shake.

'I was coming back from the village, back when things weren't so bad – when a few of us still braved going into town for supplies,' Arty said, the cockiness from his voice all gone, his tone heavy and serious. 'I was 'bout halfway back when I heard this sniffing and scratching sound in the grass to my right. Sounded big. I thought it must be a pig, or a boar, but I look around and I can't see anything. So, I follow the sound and wander off the path a little. It's getting louder and louder so I start to slow up, realising that I'm being a damned fool for straying so far from the path. Just as I'm about to turn back, I see where the noise is coming from. It looks like a big rabbit hole, or a fox's den and I breathe a bit of a sigh of relief. Then I see a nose. Just the tip of a nose sticking out the hole. Big! Big and black, with thick, wiry whiskers. A fox or a badger I think. Then it crawls out a little more and I see that it has a long, brown snout. Then, before I have a chance to think or scream or run, its head comes right out. A rat's head! A rat's head as big as a dog's, with huge black eyes staring up at me. Then I see these two hands come scratching out of the hole either side of its head. Yep! You heard me right!' he said with a nod, turning to Alexander for the first time. 'Not claws. Hands. Human hands! Pale and filthy they were and they grabbed hold of the ground in front of it and started to pull its body out. And then I did scream, and I don't mind telling that to no one because its body was that of a man. Dressed like a beggar – filthy rags from head to toe with the head of a dirty great rat, crawling its way out of its burrow towards me. I dropped the supplies I was carrying as if they were on fire and ran 'til I thought my heart would give out, and all the while I can hear scampering and sniffing and biting coming from just behind me. I never turned round to look because I knew it would be the last thing I saw if I did, so I didn't stop 'til I got back to the tavern.' He paused for a moment and took a sip of some dark liquid from a tankard. 'And that's still not the worst thing I've seen.'

A chill ran down Alexander's spine and he put down the other half of his roll, his appetite suddenly gone.

'I hope you two know what you're doing. For your sakes as much as ours!' And with that, Arty got up, finished his drink, wiped the froth from his moustache and left.

A hand suddenly grabbed Alexander's shoulder and he jumped, a little whimper escaping his lips. It was the Professor.

'Forget checking the supplies for a moment. Mr Parnell wants to give us some more information about the village. You must listen carefully. What he says may save our lives at some point. Forewarned is forearmed!' he said, and walked to the far end of the tavern. That was one of the Professor's favourite mantras. 'Forewarned is forearmed, Alexander!' along with 'Fail to prepare and prepare to fail.' After what Arty had just told him, he didn't want to prepare for anything. He just wanted to tuck himself back into bed and stay there until the Professor had finished doing whatever it was he planned to do.

He hurried after the Professor and Mr Parnell the landlord who were chatting to a group of villagers gathered around a table.

'Nathan, you should probably join us too,' Mr Parnell said to a tanned, swarthy gentleman with close-cropped hair and a scar that ran from his forehead almost around to the top of his neck. He stood up and the Professor, a tall man by anyone's standards, just came up to his shoulders. Nathan followed obediently and they made their way into a back parlour where two younger men were playing cards at the room's only table.

'We'll just be a few minutes more. I'm having quite the lucky streak,' one young man said smugly, leaning back in his chair. Nathan calmly walked over to the young man and kicked the chair out from under him, sending his cards flying into the air.

'Looks like Lady Luck just left. You'd better follow her out,' Nathan said, in a well-spoken voice that did not fit his brutish appearance. Picking the fellow up off the floor, Nathan shoved him out of the door. His card-playing companion threw his cards down in panic and hurried out the room after him.

'Well, thank you Nathan. Subtlety has never been your strong suit, has it?' Mr Parnell said, lowering himself into a chair at the far end of the table. Nathan did not reply, but sat down to one side of Mr Parnell. Alexander let the Professor sit first, then went to shut the door, the rest of the tavern staring after them. Just as the door was nearly closed it burst open again and Arty pushed his way into the room.

'If there's to be a secret meeting, I want be involved!' he bellowed, standing with his fists on his hips.

'Stone the crows, Arty, it's not a secret meeting. You're welcome to join us if you wish. We just wanted to speak where the children couldn't hear,' Mr Parnell said, exhausted with Arty already.

'Good. Well let's get started,' Arty said sitting down next to the Professor, eyeing him up and down. 'So, I guess this is the charlatan we just paid half the village's gold to?'

'Professor James Cordite at your service. And this is Alexander,' the Professor said, as way of an introduction. 'You may have met him already, maybe even helped him last night, for which I am thankful. I have been his guardian the past five years. He is my assistant and will accompany me on this contract. I realise that it may seem to you that I have charged a lot of money, but I can assure you that my fee only covers my materials, my tools, etc. I can give you the contact details of two French sisters who might consider attempting this job, but they charge at least twice as much as I do and will not do the job half as well.'

'I could have lived on that amount for a year! We don't have to listen to this. I want my money back!' Arty ranted, rising from the table.

'Sit down, Arty. We voted and decided. That part is agreed. This meeting is to tell Professor Cordite all we can to aid him in ridding Bleakhope of this evil. If you can't be of any help, get back to propping up the bar and leave us be,' Mr Parnell said, rubbing his forehead. Arty scowled and looked to Nathan for support. None came.

'Fine,' Arty said with a huff.

'Although, I must say, I didn't realise that you would be bringing a child into such danger,' Mr Parnell said, nodding in Alexander's direction.

'I will need his help. He must accompany me,' the Professor said with such finality that it looked as if Mr Parnell might just leave it at that.

'But he's just a boy. He could get hurt, or worse. Nathan here can accompany you. He has the strength of two men!' Mr Parnell said and Nathan raised one eyebrow and looked up at the Professor.

'I do not doubt his strength, or his bravery. But what I need is someone who can distil pure sulphuric acid from some very basic ingredients. I need an assistant who knows the difference between Cornswood Herb, which will rid a person of creeping paralysis and the almost identical looking Fox-Tooth weed, which will leave a person blind if eaten. But, most importantly for this mission, I need someone who can play the violin. Now, Alexander can do all this. And he does it well. So *he* accompanies me and let that be the end of it.'

Everyone turned to look Alexander up and down. He felt himself flush, his face reddening. No one said any more.

Alexander's cheeks burned long after the compliment had been paid. The Professor never gave him cheap praise. Never gave anyone any praise at all really. Although, now that Alexander thought about it, he did remember the Professor saying to him once that he made a fair cup of tea for a young man, but that really was about it. 'Praise thrown like confetti is worthless. A man should do well for himself, not to please others,' the Professor had once chided after Alexander had asked if, after performing a particularly difficult experiment to brew a sleeping draught, he had done well. So, for Alexander to hear him speak so highly of him made him want to burst into tears of happiness and rush over and hug him. Of course he did no such thing and sat in silence and hoped no one noticed how red he had gone.

'Fine. If you can vouch for his safety.'

'I do. And thank you, Mr Parnell, for trusting us to solve this most terrible of cases. When did it all begin?' the Professor asked, taking out an old, leather-bound ledger from his inside pocket and opening it on the table. He then took a quill and a small bottle of ink out of another pocket, placing them both on the table. As Nathan began to speak, the Professor opened the bottle and dipped the quill into the ink.

'It started about six months ago when a fog descended onto the village – ' Nathan began.

'Rubbish,' Arty scoffed. 'You're a fool if you think that's when it began. Strange things started when his Lordship's son disappeared last winter.' Nathan slammed his fists onto the table and began to slowly stand, glaring at Arty. 'Now I'm not saying *you're* a fool, I, I, I just meant – '

'Nathan knows what you mean, Arty. And I don't say it often, Nathan, but Arty is right about when things began,' Mr Parnell said, putting a hand on Nathan's arm. Nathan stared at the hand that held him back for a moment then settled back into his seat. Arty exhaled the breath he had been holding, relieved to have avoided what was sure to have been a very short confrontation with Nathan. 'It did all start when Lord Bleakhope's son, Master Edgar, disappeared – '

'How old was his son Edgar?' the Professor interrupted.

'He was just five years old,' Mr Parnell replied. 'Such a sweet boy. When he disappeared, his father near bankrupted the household. Spent every penny they had hiring soldiers and trackers and poachers to find him. Old Dan, the barman here, and his family are the best trackers in the county, but there was simply no sign of him. They never found so much as a hair. It was as if he had just vanished. Having lost his wife the year before as well, it was all too much for his mind to take. He hid himself away.'

'Then the mist came,' Nathan continued.

'No. Not quite. Then Lord Bleakhope couldn't afford to keep his staff on. Had to let them all go – all of them except for this new doctor that showed up. He stayed on. There are rumours he convinced Lord Bleakhope that he could bring his son back somehow,' Mr Parnell continued.

'Right. So Lord Bleakhope's son disappeared, a strange man arrived, Lord Bleakhope dismissed all the staff, then the mist came,' Nathan tried again. There were nods from all around the table. 'Then other people started going missing.'

'Who?' the Professor said, dipping his quill into the ink pot again. 'I will need names, occupations, descriptions.'

'Well, the first to go missing after Lord Bleakhope's son Edgar was little Bobby Quinn. He was only a wee lad, nine years old or such. Thin as a stick. Is that the kind of thing you wanted?' Nathan asked.

'Perfect. Where was he last seen?'

'The night he went missing he went to go fishing by the lake before the sun went down, right around supper time. Never came back. Then Lucy went missing, Old Dan's daughter. She was as good a tracker as her uncles were and she was looking for Bobby in the orchard when she was last seen, but she never came home,' Nathan continued.

'Description?' the Professor simply asked.

'Older girl, almost a woman I suppose. Auburn hair. Kind hearted. Never troubled no one.'

'Then my Sarah, my wife disappeared,' Nathan said coldly. 'We were all still living in the village then. She went out to fetch water from the well. Never returned. I looked everywhere. Not a sign.'

'Aye. He looked non-stop for two whole days. By the time he stopped two more people had vanished,' Mr Parnell said. 'After that the order becomes a bit of a blur. But we know that before this nightmare began, the village, plus those at Bleakhope Manor, the two farms and out here as far as the tavern, was home to three hundred and twenty-seven people. Only fifty-eight of us remain.'

Alexander gasped.

'Now, not all of those unaccounted for have vanished by any means,' Mr Parnell continued. 'Most people went to live with family in neighbouring villages. Some of the younger folk, who didn't have relatives nearby, went to find work in one of the big towns further south. But a lot, maybe even as many as twenty men, women and children have vanished.' Mr Parnell shook his head solemnly and stared at his own hands which were clenched on the table in front of him. 'As each person went missing the mist grew thicker and the sightings began. Shadows and giant creatures. It was the unknown that terrified us. We never knew what would be waiting for us out in the fog.'

'And how many have been killed?' the Professor asked, turning to a new page in his ledger.

'It's hard to say,' Mr Parnell replied. 'We never recover the bodies. Often there are just ... ' he paused, thinking how best to phrase it, ' ... signs of a struggle. Quite often there is nothing at all. People are taken in some quite terrifying and violent ways, but there is never any body to be found when we go to search the next afternoon when it's lighter. Not even any blood. Not normally.'

'Give me an example,' the Professor asked. Mr Parnell was about to begin, but he caught the Professor's eye and nodded in Alexander's direction.

'Should I tell you after?' Mr Parnell said, and Alexander realised Mr Parnell was trying to shelter him from another horror story.

'Nonsense. Alex is going out with me tomorrow. Forewarned is forearmed.'

Alexander nodded and tried to smile his appreciation to the Professor. The truth was that he would have been quite happy for them to talk about this after he had gone. Ignorance is bliss, Alexander thought to himself. Ever heard of that saying, Professor?

'Fine. The last person to go missing was Jeremiah. Six of us had headed over to the woodshed, just past the orchard on the edge of the village. We have plentiful supplies of wood here for a normal summer, but the nights get so unseasonably cold and there are so many of us here now that the wood reserves were running low. We started to stock up our bags. No horse will venture there now so we have to carry everything ourselves. It was dark and misty, but things were going well until a deafening screech cried out above us. We were all blown off our feet by a sudden gust of wind, mist swirling all around us and we saw – ' he paused and shook his head as if he didn't believe what he was saying, ' – we thought we saw a bird swoop down in the darkness and take Jeremiah.'

'And Jeremiah was a full-grown man?' the Professor asked, not patronisingly or accusingly, simply clarifying a fact.

'Aye, not a small man neither,' Nathan said, taking over the story. 'Whatever took him, and I never saw it properly either, must have been huge. All I saw were these two amber eyes cutting through the mist above me. I felt a burning across my head and then it was gone. If it wasn't for this scar I wouldn't even believe it myself,' he finished, running a finger over the angry red stripe that went from between his eyebrows to the back of his head like half a red crown.

There was a strained quiet after they had finished their story. The only sound was the Professor's quill scratching over the dry pages.

'Right, thank you gentlemen for your time. Alexander and myself will need to get prepared,' the Professor said, recorking his tiny ink bottle and wiping its edges with a cloth.

'Did you not just hear what we said?' Arty shouted and leapt up, sending his chair toppling backwards behind him. 'Some hellish creature snatched a full-grown man from out of the mist. I've been chased by a man with the head of a rat. Others have seen tree roots drag a man under the soil! What's in your luggage that is going to stop that, huh? What can you and this boy,' he said pointing at Alexander, his finger only a few inches from his face, 'this boy, who is wetter than the clothes he fainted in, do?'

'I blacked-out, I never fainted,' Alexander muttered weakly.

'What are you going to do to stop that?' Arty continued, ignoring Alexander's interjection.

The Professor calmly blew on the ink on his ledger, not shutting it until he was sure it was dry. He dabbed at the page with the corner of his cloth, inspected it and closed his ledger, tucking it into an inside pocket of his jacket.

'I know you are scared. It is natural to be scared of what we do not understand. I can assure you though, whatever dark agent is pulling the strings behind this, we will find them and put an end to this. There is much to be hopeful about, Arty. I predict that within the week, your village will have returned to the quaint, rustic village that it was just last year. I will also have returned some, if not all, of your missing,' the Professor said and rose from his seat.

There was a moment of silence from everyone who sat around the table. Mr Parnell looked around at Arty's and Nathan's stunned faces which reflected his own awed shock and disbelief.

'Are you serious?' Mr Parnell asked.

'I assume that is a rhetorical question. You did pay me to save your village did you not? A task that I agreed to do, and when I agree to do something, you can rest assured it will be done,' he said and nodded to them. 'Now, if you will excuse us, Alexander and I have much to prepare. We shall meet again tonight after supper where I will tell you more. I will set out late this afternoon to confirm my theory. If I am right, I may even return with the first of the missing.' And with this, the Professor tucked his chair under the table and left the room.

3

The Stable

ALEXANDER IMMEDIATELY FELT STUPID THAT HE had not followed the Professor out of the room straight away, but the truth was, he was too awestuck to move too.

Smiling stupidly at them, he stood and tucked his own chair under the table, jogging everyone's drinks as he did so, shattering their shocked silence.

'Be careful boy!' Arty shouted, stepping back from the table and wiping the froth from his spilt drink off his legs.

'Sorry! Sorry about that,' Alexander said as he backed out of the room, his face flushing red again. Once outside the room, he closed the door behind him and breathed a sigh of relief. Then he looked up and saw the whole tavern staring at him. He grinned, waved and made his way across the tavern to the curving staircase on the far side. At the top of the stairs he saw the Professor standing thoughtfully outside the room Alexander had woken up in.

'Is it possible? What they're describing I mean?'

'Not just possible but certain, I am afraid. I hope you are

mentally ready for what this week will hold. Your courage will be seriously tested, as will your resourcefulness and your logic,' the Professor said and opened the door for him to enter. Alexander went in and sat on the corner of his bed, the mattress sagging under him. As he sat there, the Professor began to pace up and down the small room, his hands first clasped behind his back and then, as if in prayer, pointed beneath his chin. This went on for quite some time and anyone who did not know the Professor might have asked if he was alright. Alexander knew better than to interrupt his thought process though and stayed quiet, thinking over the conversations downstairs himself.

'Conclusions, Alex? What is your theory of these strange goings on?'

Alexander was fully prepared for this question. The Professor would often ask him to work through a problem logically. Not, Alexander supposed, because the Professor would find his answers enlightening, but this was all part of his tutelage: helping Alexander to refine his thinking, helping him to work things through.

'Well. Based on what I have seen and heard already, I would say that this is directly related to Lord Bleakhope and, in particular, to the day his son disappeared. They said that the other disappearances began after his death.'

'A logical supposition based on the facts that you have at your disposal. Go on,' the Professor waved. Alexander hadn't thought through much more than this, but he kept talking and hoped that it would lead somewhere.

'The man that arrived at the manor house sounds suspicious,

well his timing does at least. Also, no one has been found dead, well, not wholly dead, which means that they may well be using the bodies. If they were just killed or even eaten or devoured in some way there would be more remains or blood. Perhaps they are taking and using the villagers somehow.'

'That is perceptive,' the Professor said as he paced back and forth listening intently. Two separate compliments in one day, Alexander thought to himself. If he had to put the events of the last few days in order of the strange and unusual, he would put being complimented twice by the Professor slightly above being chased by shadows through the mist. 'Can you tell me what they are being used for?'

Alexander simply shook his head.

'An unfair question perhaps because I have seen something like this in a village in India. Nothing to this scale though.' The Professor looked back to Alexander and obviously saw his polite confusion. 'I will be able to reveal more to you in time once we have tested my theory this afternoon. But I cannot say too much yet. What I can share with you though is the very edges of the science behind what is going on here. A science that your father and I had studied in-depth as purely theoretical. But it seems as though someone has turned theory into a very dark reality.

'As you know, during my studies at university, and for a long while afterwards, my curiosity for the strange and unexplained grew until it took over my every waking thought. I kept this quiet of course. The fellows at Oxbridge would not have condoned such base and worthless studies, even though I conducted my studies to the same rigorous standards for which others held me in such high regard. So, I kept my passion private, buying up books on ghosts, hauntings, strange happenings and elusive creatures, never daring to read them in public. It was not until I met your father that I ever spoke of it to another soul. But then in your father I found my own passion reflected back. We would meet up and theorise and speculate and argue about scientific explanations for that which could not be explained.' The Professor sat down on the edge of one of the other beds in the corner by the window and stared out across the misty moors and back in time.

'How can you explain some of the strange creatures that have been sighted across the world? How can no less than eight different farmers on eight different occasions in a village in India see a flying creature the size and shape of a man with the wings of a giant moth swoop down and steal cattle. How can a giant cat the size of a sheep terrorize a whole village in France? Well, we did come to a theory. A theory that could explain all of these things and countless more besides. We theorised that there must exist a world similar to our own, a world that held many creatures that were both strange and terrifying to us. Our two worlds existed without our knowing about the other, however sometimes, for reasons we did not fully understand then, things would pass from their world to ours and vice versa.

'At the time, our experiments proved fruitless and we began to run out of what little funding we could gather. Now, however, I think someone,' and he paused here for a curiously long time, 'has found a way.'

Alexander nodded, contemplating a shadow world like their own, existing parallel to this one.

'Still, I will explain more once I have tested a hypothesis tomorrow.'

Alexander knew there would be no point in trying to argue with this. As the Professor had already stated, if he said he was going to do or not do something, then he would not change his mind for anything.

'You have a few hours to prepare some materials for us,' said the Professor and he handed Alexander a piece of parchment with a neatly written list. 'Everything you should need is in the trunks. The compound on the list must be made exactly to my instructions. Also, you'll need to tune your violin', and he indicated the luggage in the corner of the room that he had brought up. 'You can also stretch your legs and wander around the tavern. I'm sure that I do not need to stress that leaving the tavern is strictly forbidden.' Alexander had no desire to leave the tavern whatsoever. 'I shall be preparing a few things myself. I shall see you after lunch if you do not need me for anything this morning. If you do require me for anything, I shall be up on the next floor. Mr Parnell has given me use of a larger room to myself. I'm afraid you will have to share your room with a few of the villagers. Make sure they don't go prodding around our luggage.' With this, the Professor nodded a goodbye and left the room.

Alexander sighed and looked at the list that the Professor had given him. It seemed simple enough. There were some medicinal elixirs that were a bit fiddly to make, and a formula for a compound that he was unfamiliar with, but he thought it shouldn't take too long. Opening all the chests, and reminding himself of their contents, he set to work.

In the end, he estimated that it took him three hours, although with no clock and no clue as to where the sun was, it could have been longer. The compound was new to him and took a lot longer than he thought to make up. It required extremely precise amounts of a number of rare substances that they had brought along and some of the ingredients left Alexander feeling very uncomfortable about what the compound's eventual use could be. Chromite shavings – not an easy thing to shave Alexander discovered, powdered glass and a number of crystal fragments were just a few of the more unusual ingredients. He packed all the materials neatly away and locked the cases, pushing the ones under his bed that would fit.

A feeling of claustrophobia began to descend on him and he felt he had to get out of the room. He made his way back out onto the landing and surveyed his options. A little way to his right were the stairs that led back down to the main room. To his left were three other doors, one next to his room and two opposite. At the far end of the corridor was another set of stairs that led upwards. Alexander decided to go back downstairs. He didn't want to be stared at again, but he was beginning to feel hungry and had no idea what he was supposed to do about lunch. Did he have to pay? He only had a few coins on him, but maybe the Professor had started an account.

'Excuse me?' Alexander asked when he made his way through the cold stares of the main room. 'I would love some lunch, but I only have a few coppers.' He tried to look as pathetic as possible, not a hard job Alexander suspected, as most people had watched him fainting and bumbling around for the past day. He had hoped the bartender would take pity on him and insist Alexander put his money away, but all the bartender did was stare at the coins in Alexander's hand as if he had shown him a lump of manure.

'Well, you're gonna be very hungry then, aren't you?' the bartender said in a gruff snort and wandered down to the other end of the bar where he rolled his eyes to another man.

'I can help cook. Or clean. I can sweep up and keep the fire going. I'll work for my lunch,' Alexander called after him. The bartender looked him up and down as if contemplating what work he could put him to.

'Okay. I've got some cleaning jobs you can do for your lunch,' he said with a wry smile and indicated for Alexander to follow with a little tilt of his head.

He followed the bartender, who was wiping his hands on an already filthy apron, behind the bar and through a narrow passage. Along the corridor a few barrels and bottles in crates stood stacked up against the bare, stone walls. The passage had four or five other passageways and staircases leading off it and Alexander began to appreciate just what a huge building this was. They went down a set of narrow stone steps and the bartender pushed one half of a set of double doors open and they walked out into a small courtyard that must have sat in the centre of the inn. Alexander looked up at the old building, with its skeleton of black timbers supporting the whitewashed plaster and then up to the highest room where he saw the Professor for a brief moment at the window. Alexander went to wave, but the Professor had already turned away and disappeared from view.

As they walked across the courtyard Alexander thought it might have been a beautiful place to sit in the summer with the sun gleaming off the walls, the green of the grass below and the blue sky above. But the grass was mud, the sky was slate grey and the walls were damp with mist.

They went through another set of thick wooden doors and into a stable. It stank. It smelt as if it hadn't been cleaned out in weeks.

'It hasn't been cleaned out in weeks,' the bartender said. 'The young lad who used to keep it clean packed his bags and headed south. We only had two horses left, but your horses turned up this morning. If they had had any sense they would have run a hundred miles in any direction, but horses are loyal. Stupid and loyal. So, they need mucking out and fresh straw put down.'

'Wait, I didn't catch your name,' Alexander called out.

'The folks here call me Old Dan, but you can call me Sir.'

Alexander remembered what Mr Parnell had said earlier that day about Old Dan. 'I was sorry to hear about your daughter's disappearance, Sir.'

The bartender stared at him for a moment then left without another word.

Alexander had never mucked horses out before, but he was used to hard work, so he threw himself into the task of raking up the old straw and manure and piling it into the barrows. The horses paid him little attention but seemed skittish, shuffling about and pulling at the reins that were tied to a beam that ran across the back wall. The hard work was not the difficult part, it was the smell that slowed him down. It was horrendous and reminded Alexander of neat ammonia. He covered his nose and mouth with his shirt as he worked and began to feel lightheaded, loading the manure and wet straw into the two wooden wheelbarrows. He opened the doors to the front of the stable to let some fresher air in, frightened he might pass out in the rank odours of the place, but the dank and fetid air outside offered no relief. He needed to unload the now full barrows somewhere and get rid of the smell. He saw what he was looking for – a manure heap not too far away from the inn. The steaming mound was silhouetted in the mist about forty yards away. If he ran, he could make it to the manure heap and back to the safety of the tavern in under twenty seconds. Pushing a full barrow could take double that though and he would have to make two trips. That was two trips more than he wanted to take. The Professor had specifically told him that leaving the tavern was strictly forbidden but Alexander had made a deal with Old Dan. Professor Cordite would look very unfavourably if he did a sloppy job or failed in a task he had promised to complete. It would reflect badly on the Professor and his work here. Besides, if he did it quickly, he wouldn't need to know.

Edging the barrow to the open doors he looked around. He could still see the manure pile forty or so yards away, a darker grey against the mist. There were very few sounds – the occasional voice could be heard from way back in the tavern, but he couldn't make out the words. Outside, it was windless and silent. He stared for a long time into the fog looking for the deformed and misshapen shadows that had chased him the day before, but there was nothing. Alexander's hands grew clammy on the barrow's handles and he wiped them on his shirt and took a deep breath, sweat beading on his forehead. He was reminded of a time a few years back, one summer when he and some other boys from school stood on the edge of an old quarry that had filled with water. It was a spot that they had gone to swim in often, even though they were frequently warned how dangerous it was. It was a ritual, a rite of passage, to climb to this one point on the man-made cliff face and jump out over the rocks into the clear water below. He had stood there, his toes over the edge of the cliff like his toes were peeking out of the tavern and into the outside now – sweaty hands and pounding heart. And just like then, he knew if he tarried any longer he would lose his courage, so he stopped thinking about it and started to run.

Sprinting across the flat dirt just outside the tavern was easy. The barrow ran smooth and true but when he hit the rougher ground the wheelbarrow wobbled and threatened to tip as it bounced across the tufts of damp, yellowing grass. He managed to keep it upright, but it meant having to almost stop. His eyes darted around looking for black shapes moving from out of the grey towards him, but everything was eerily still. Picking up the pace again he made it to the manure heap. Steam was still rising from the waste and he dumped the straw, turned the barrow in a narrow arc and began to run, but not before some movement from the pile of filth caught his eye. He didn't dare stop and stare though and ran back as fast as the cart could travel. He didn't stop until he slammed into the far wall of the stable.

He sank down, his hands on his knees, and stayed there breathing heavily, the horses staring at him as if he was mad. Eventually he pulled himself up and looked at the remaining barrow of old straw and manure. Old Dan must have known he would have to take the waste outside. Maybe Old Dan wanted to put him in danger, Alexander thought. Or maybe Old Dan thought he would be too scared and that he would refuse. The idea steeled him somewhat. He liked to prove people wrong. Taking hold of the second barrow he wheeled it to the stable doors. His own heart thumping away was the only sound now and he willed it to be quiet. He imagined it like a drum, echoing out to things that crawled in the shadows beyond the mist. Come eat, the drum beat was saying. Here is warm, pumping blood, just follow the drum beat. He was overthinking again, so he ran. This time he anticipated the rough ground and slowed down a step or two before he hit it, managing to keep the wheelbarrow from toppling. His own panting, the squeaking of the barrow and the thudding of the wheel over the ground meant that hearing anything approaching was impossible. He tried to make up for it by frantically looking about as he ran. Closing the last agonising yards to the manure heap he began to tip out the straw. That's when he saw the movement again from the middle of the mound of rotting filth, and heard the horrible squelching, slurping noises.

Crawling out from the steaming brown waste was a maggot as long as his forearm. A pale, flabby maggot with a puckered mouth that opened and closed with a sucking, gulping sound. It wriggled and reared up like a snake. Alexander was frozen, unable to tear his eyes away from the abomination. Then the whole heap of waste started to move and squirm and other maggots wriggled out of the filth and rose up to face him, each one over a foot long.

Alexander turned and ran, abandoning the wheelbarrow. A noise rose up behind him – first as a faint hum, then as an angry buzzing just above him. He had made it halfway back when the first fly crashed into his face. He turned towards the buzzing and only had time to register its grotesque size before it smacked into the side of his face. Two giant, dull eyes as big as dishes and hairy legs as thick as his fingers but twice as long. It was as if he had been punched across the temple. Alexander instinctively tried to swat it away after it had struck him and he caught it hard enough so that it fell to the ground just in front of his feet where he accidently stepped on it with a crack and a crunch that made him sick. He spat the bile that rose into his mouth, swatting away at the sound of buzzing near his ear as the giant flies tried to land on him. He pushed a massive fly off instinctively as it landed on his shoulder, and sprinted through the stable's doors, and he didn't look back until he was across the stable and slamming the inner door shut behind him.

Panting, he leant against the door with all his might until his breathing began to slow down. Then he was sick again. After a few minutes he stood up straight, shook himself out and opened the door an inch. The four horses shifted about uncomfortably, but there were no sign of the flies. He opened the door a little more so that he could fit his head through and look around. It didn't look as if the flies had passed the door. It was as if there was something about the tavern that was keeping them back.

Once Alexander was sure that there were no more giant insects, he mopped up his own sick, shut the stable doors as quickly as he could and went to find the bartender.

Old Dan was behind the bar, leaning against its polished oak surface and talking to two men.

'So,' Old Dan said when he saw Alexander walk in. 'You cleaned that stable out yet?' he asked with a dry smile.

'Yes, good as new,' Alexander said, trying to come off as carefree.

'And what about the old straw. You got rid of that?'

'Yep,' he replied with a casual smile.

'What? You took it out to the manure pile?' Old Dan asked, clearly shocked.

'Yes. I had to do a few trips because it was in quite a state. It was nice to get a bit of air actually, the smell got pretty bad in there at times.'

Old Dan just stared at him for a moment, then laughed. First only a chuckle, then a bellow. 'You're alright, boy,' he said, slapping Alexander on the back. 'It gets pretty scary out in the mist, don't it?'

Now Alexander laughed too. 'To be honest, it was terrifying out there,' he said, and Old Dan nodded.

'Yeah, well, I didn't think you'd do it. Thought you'd pee yourself and come running back in here crying. You've got some guts,' he said with a smile. 'I'll make you some lunch. The Professor has already paid for all your meals.'

'What? You mean I didn't have to clean the stable out! Why didn't you tell me?' Alexander said, anger creeping into his voice.

Old Dan laughed again and turned to head into the kitchen.

'What fun would that have been?' he chuckled.

To be fair to Old Dan, Alexander thought, he managed to make a pretty good meal with provisions that must have been running low. He had brought Alexander out a sausage stew with a crusty roll that all tasted as good as it smelt.

'Where do you get your fresh bread from? Is the mill still running?' Alexander called out from his table to Old Dan who was wiping down the bar.

'No, lad. The mill was abandoned some months back. Well, something lives there now, but it ain't human. So we take it in turns to ride out to the next village. We go in threes and fours, sell what we still have left to sell and bring back what we can. The other villages have been good to us. They don't charge us more than cost. But every journey we take gets more dangerous. Most times now we have to turn back.' Alexander must have visibly shaken his head. 'This is our home, we can't just abandon it. Where's home for you, lad?'

Alexander thought about the question for a moment. 'London some months, Bath, Oxford, Cambridge at other times. Wherever the Professor is called to. He goes where he is needed and takes me with him.' Alexander saw his quizzical look and saw he would have to elaborate further. 'The Professor and my father wanted to be famous scientists and explorers when they were younger. That was a dream that got my father killed. The Professor told me that after my father died he was offered the deanship of the University of Berlin a few weeks later but he turned it down to take me on. He sacrificed his dreams to look after me. My father let his obsession kill him, whereas the Professor threw it all away for me. I guess home is wherever he is now.'

Old Dan shook his head, and walked away. 'No life for a boy.'

Alexander carried on eating in silence, contemplating this, when the Professor walked in.

'Time we ventured outside, Alex.'

4

The Farm

'IS THE COMPOUND PREPARED TO MY specifications?' the Professor asked Alexander.

'Yes,' Alexander said, showing the Professor the large glass tube with the black powder in it.

'And do you have your violin? Is it tuned?'

'Yes,' he replied, knowing the Professor must have a good reason for him to need his violin. He hoped he wouldn't be serenading shadow monsters and rat men until they surrendered.

'Good, then let us set out.'

Professor Cordite pulled his long leather coat tightly around him and pulled his tricorn hat down at the front. They left through the main entrance with their packs, Alexander with his violin in its black leather case across his shoulder, and the Professor with a crossbow across his. Alexander knew which he'd rather be carrying when it came to a fight.

Stepping away from the tavern felt to Alexander like it might feel if you were swimming away from a lifeboat when lost at sea. The villagers might have been strange and unwelcoming, but it was still a constant torch in the darkness, a refuge. Looking back as they walked away, the tavern's lights were slowly eaten up by the mist until they vanished altogether. After the gravel of the track around the tavern, the ground they walked on turned slimy as the grass had begun to rot. They had not travelled very far, but the tavern felt like a world away now and the little voice of panic was whispering to him to run back.

Halfway across the field Alexander stopped next to a life-size crucifix about as big as the ones they had in most parish churches.

'Professor, why is there a crucifix here?' The Professor stopped and stared at it long and hard.

'It's not a crucifix, well, not exactly,' he said after a while. 'They are the poles used to support a scarecrow.'

'So where is the scarecrow?' Alexander asked. They both looked around. Nothing but mist crept about them.

'I don't know. But we should keep moving. Across this next field is the orchard where I hope we will find what we are looking for,' the Professor said.

'And what is that exactly?'

'A doorway or a portal of some kind to the other world. I don't know what it will look like because I've only worked it out as an equation. I can show the mathematical calculations if that helps?' Alexander shook his head. That would not have helped. 'You will know it when you see it. Somehow, I theorise, the villagers are being used to hold doors open between worlds. Again, I do not know how, we will have to see. But when we find them I will shake some of the compound into the air. The mixture you have prepared for me, when exposed to a low frequency – that is where your violin playing comes in – will vibrate and temporarily close any portal or doorway. Again, I can show you the mathematical calculations for this if it helps.'

'Maybe later,' Alexander said, just trying not to fall over the uneven ground.

They got close to the edge of the first field where it dipped into a ditch before rising again on the other side. A noise made them both turn about. Stumbling over the ridges and troughs of the ploughed field, four people staggered slowly towards them.

'Who are they, Professor?' Alexander asked, taking a step backwards. The Professor stared for a second longer.

'Not who – what.'

Alexander looked again and froze. The creatures were not human. He could see now that their heads were made from hessian sacks and straw. Their hands were made from twigs – scarecrows.

'Wickermen. Shamblemen – living scarecrows. Straw bodies inhabited by shadows,' the Professor said quickly, shaking his head as if unable to believe what he was seeing. 'I have read about them, but to see them!' The Professor sounded almost in awe of what was staggering towards him. 'Quickly, light torches!'

The Professor's curt command snapped Alexander out of his shock and he opened the bag, grabbing two short metal poles that were wrapped at the head in oilcloth. He laid them on the cold earth and frantically snatched up the box of matches – all the while the wickermen were shambling close enough so that he could smell their stale, rotting stench. His shaking hands opened the matchbox, spilling the contents everywhere. He grabbed a match and struck it on the side of the box. The match snapped. He grabbed at another – the wickermen were just a few yards away now. He looked up at them, the match shaking between his fingers, and he could not look away. Their faces were a mess of straw and sackcloth with hollows for eyes and a mouth. They were horrific, and they were nearly on top of him.

'Light them, Alex!' the Professor shouted. Alexander stared down at the match in his numb fingers. He struck it and the match flared into life. He held it to one of the torches which caught aflame and he passed it to the Professor. The Professor shook his head. 'You hold it, distract them. Keep them away from me as long as you can. I have to look for the door.' Without another word, the Professor ran off into the fog.

Alexander turned to the approaching wickermen who were now looming above him, their straw legs struggling across the rough ground – their long, twig hands almost dragging along next to them. Stumbling backwards he swung the torch at them. 'Get back!' he said, the words half lost behind the lump in his throat. The hideous scarecrows kept coming though and now their foul smell filled his senses – a mouldy, rotting reek that rose above the burning paraffin torch. Their putrid odour and the fear that gripped his stomach made him sick and Alexander staggered further back, the torch held between his two shaking hands. One of the shamblemen lurched forward, its thorny hands grabbing for him. Alexander stabbed the torch into its straw head and it fell back silently, its face smouldering. The scarecrow steadied itself and then lunged forward again wrapping its twig hands around Alexander's left arm. He screamed out in fear and pain as thorns dug into his skin. He stabbed at it again, this time plunging the flaming torch deep into its torso. It tore away, the torch still burning its innards, lighting it up from the inside. A nest of sharp sticks which had been its hand still clung to Alexander's arm, squeezing. Alexander ran with it still attached, still clawing at him. At that moment he didn't care if he was leading them all straight back to the Professor, he just had to get away.

The violin and his backpack slowed him down, banging against his back as he ran, but he was still faster than the shamblemen. Disorientated, Alexander stopped running and looked around. He didn't know where he was in relation to the tavern and that terrified him. He looked up from his arm as he pulled the last of the scarecrow's twig hand off himself and dropped it to the ground where it lay twitching. Black, withered trees, all in neat rows, stretched out in front of him. It was the orchard. He was quite sure he would be no safer in there but he knew he couldn't go back into the mist across the fields for fear of running into more scarecrows so he made his way into the orchard and it brought a whole new terror.

It was much easier to walk on the flat ground of the orchard, but he knew that anything could be hiding behind any one of the trees, just waiting for him. Walking between the rows of skeletal trees constantly expecting something to jump out on him was unbearable. His pace began to slow as he edged around every tree expecting a scarecrow or a man with a rat's head to leap at him.

He had walked far enough now that when he looked around

him there were rows of trees in all directions vanishing into the mist and he soon became unsure of which way he had come. That was when he heard it. A deep snorting sound from the fog in front of him. For a second he froze until the sound came again. It sounded like the snorting of a bull. Quickly, Alexander grabbed hold of the branches above him and pulled himself up into the tree. The branches were wet and greasy which made climbing hard, but he scrambled up as high as he could and waited. A large shadow began to appear from the fog and Alexander thought that it *was* a bull, but as it slowly emerged from the mist, Alexander could see that it was no creature he had ever seen before. It had the barrel-shaped body of a bull, stocky and muscular, but it had six legs instead of four. Its head was more like that of a horse, a long snout with two protruding teeth or tusks. All Alexander could do was stare in awe as the giant beast continued to lumber past just a few yards below and slowly disappear in the mist behind him again.

'I've found it! Alex, I've found it!' Alexander heard the Professor's voice call through the fog not too far away. At the sound of the Professor's voice, a wave of relief washed over him and he breathed out, not knowing how long he had been holding his breath for. He panicked then, wanting the Professor to stay silent now so as not to attract the attention of this new creature. Alexander was quite certain he wouldn't be able to outrun whatever that thing was. 'Alex, quickly!' the Professor's voice came again. Alexander wanted to go to him – he never liked to keep the Professor waiting, but his legs just didn't want to move. He hugged one of the branches tighter, his whole body trembling.

Now he was safe up there, he didn't want to get down. He felt himself moving and thought he must be fainting or getting dizzy but it wasn't him that was moving, it was the tree. The branch he was clinging to was slowly curling back whilst the other branches were closing in on him. Before he could process what was happening, the branches had wrapped around his legs and had begun to knot around his waist. He tried to slip down through the branches, but he was being squeezed too tight and he would never be able to get his backpack and violin off in time. He grabbed a branch above him and tried to pull himself up. His hands slipped on the greasy bark but he manged to finally get a grip, digging his nails into the soft bark and pulling himself up. His legs slid free. As he pulled himself out of the branches the tree seemed to sense it and reached up towards him. Alexander jumped, leaping away from the tree. The ground came rushing up to meet him and he landed with a thud, the wind knocked out of him. As he rolled onto all fours, trying desperately to get his breath back, he heard creaking from all around him. The other trees were slowly moving his way, their branches curling out towards him. He scrambled up, swinging his violin case back over his shoulder. He ran towards where he had heard the Professor's voice, wheezing for air. After a few seconds the trees grew still again and he stopped to look back, his hands on his knees. The trees behind him swayed, but only as if there had been a breeze.

'Alex!' The cry came again loud and clear. A few seconds more of pained jogging and Alexander found the Professor standing in front of a massive tree that was ebony black and thicker than an oak. It was not a tree from Earth, at least the Earth he knew.

'That is what we are looking for!' the Professor said, and pointed. Alexander looked and it took his brain a while to process what he saw. There was another world in front of him – at least a patch of it. Beyond the mist of his own world glimmered another world with thick, black plants that could not have been from Earth. It was like the entrance to a tunnel or the mouth of a cave, a doorway to another realm just in front of him – and there, under a cascade of mist, was the ghost of a girl. She was close in age to him, curled up in the hollow of the tree, half in this world and half in the other. It was as if she was the reflection of a girl in a dull pool. Her image was at moments clear and vivid, the next it shimmered and almost vanished. She was sitting up, with her arms pulling her legs close to her, her red hair frozen in time across her body.

'Who is she?'

'Old Dan's daughter, if I am not mistaken,' the Professor said, kneeling down and taking out the concoction that Alexander had made earlier that day.

'What's wrong with her? Is she a ghost?'

'A power unknown to me has frozen her life-force. She is no longer of this world,' the Professor said matter-of-factly.

'She's dead?' Alexander asked.

'No. Trapped between worlds. She is being used as a key. When a key is in a door, it is neither fully one side nor the other. Neither is it fully between rooms either. She is being used to hold the doorway open between our world and this other.'

'Then we have to pull her out,' Alexander said, stepping forward. The Professor, still kneeling, held out a hand in front of him.

'Don't get too close. This portal is how those creatures pass into our world. I am hoping that when we close it, every dark thing here will return to that other world. But I do not know. If you stumble into their world, I am not sure I could get you back.'

'But what about her?' Alexander said, pointing to the girl.

'She is not fully in their world or ours but I have a plan to get her back. Get your violin out of its case. I need you to play me the lowest note you can and hold it for as long as you can,' the Professor said.

Opening the case's three catches, Alexander took out his violin, confused, but not prepared to question the Professor. His violin was a simple instrument of spruce and maple, chipped and scratched in places, but well loved. He set the violin's rest on his shoulder and positioned his fingers. Raising his elbow higher than the violin, he pressed down hard on the strings using his index finger to guide the bow across them. A perfect low G note rang out around them.

From the fog to his left he heard something coming. A second later four dark silhouettes appeared in the fog.

'Professor, the shamblemen are back!' Alexander cried out, the note cut short as he took a step back. Opening the bottle, the Professor tipped a small amount of the compound Alexander had made into his own hand and threw it into the air.

'Play!' the Professor ordered. Alexander started playing again as the living scarecrows shuffled forwards, their hideous faces twisted in spite, their thorny twig hands outstretched. The note's echo grew louder and the air seemed to fizz and vibrate in reaction to the violin. The whole area around them began to shake. Everything – every particle around them shimmered and shook as the portal between the two worlds pulsed. The shamblemen were only a few yards away now. Alexander just wanted to drop the violin and run but he kept playing. There was a cracking sound and the shamblemen and the porthole to the other world all disappeared. Even most of the mist seemed to sink into the ground and vanish. The girl was suddenly there though, truly there. Her hair was a bright red, not the partial fog and smoke as it had seemed before.

'We did it! Is she alright?' Alexander asked, staring at the girl.

'I do not know yet. I do not know how she was frozen like that, but we have to get her back to the tavern,' the Professor said, lifting her over his shoulder effortlessly. Alexander packed his violin away and placed the glass jar containing the compound back in his pack.

Not all the mist had disappeared in some places, but a gentle breeze was rising and the fog was starting to clear.

'Is it over?' Alexander asked, enjoying the warmth that was carried with the breeze on his face.

'No. She is just one key of many. But we have struck back. We must find all the keys and close all the portals to the other world. They will know we are here now,' the Professor said, striding ahead with Alexander struggling to keep up. He had to take two hasty steps to each of Professor Cordite's. 'Things will only get more difficult.'

'Oh good,' Alexander said. 'Who are *they* anyway?'

The Professor bit his bottom lip as he walked.

'I am not entirely sure. But he – they – have an advanced knowledge of removing the barriers between our worlds.' Alexander knew that when the Professor said he was not entirely sure that it really meant he was almost certain but wasn't ready to share.

With the mist almost cleared they could see the tavern easily now and they corrected their course to head in the right direction. Looking back, Alexander could see the village of Bleakhope and the surrounding areas were still covered with fog. They had cleared a huge section of mist, but four-fifths of the land was still covered in a veil of grey.

Their boots scraped on the gravel path as they approached the tavern and they saw faces appear at the small windows. Alexander hammered on the large oak doors which were answered immediately. The whole room stared at the entrance in silence as Alexander entered. Then the Professor stepped inside next to Alexander and the room erupted in sound and movement. People rushed forward to take the girl from the Professor's arms and they carried her to a hastily cleared table.

'Lucy!' Old Dan cried, pushing his way out from behind the bar to rush over to her. 'Is she dead? Is she alright?'

The room still rang with people's gasps and mutterings. There was a subdued excitement in the air. People stared at each other wide eyed, wanting to celebrate the return of one of their own, but not sure if she was alive.

'She's alive,' the Professor said, and an awed hush fell on

everyone as they listened to the man who had brought her home. He took his tricorn hat off and wiped the sweat off his brow. 'There is nothing physically wrong with her, but she has been through a terrible ordeal. Goodness knows what horrors she has seen. I am hoping with rest and food she will make a swift recovery. You should get her to bed somewhere comfortable where you can watch over her.'

Old Dan nodded and wiped a tear from his eye. With Nathan helping to clear a path through the villagers, Old Dan scooped her up and carried her upstairs.

Mr Parnell made his way over to the Professor and vigorously shook his hand. 'I knew you could do it, Professor! I just knew it.'

'We need to talk,' the Professor said, pulling the shorter man to one side. He nodded towards the back room and made his way over there indicating for Alexander to follow as well. Alexander shut the door behind him and sat down in the same chair he had before. Before the Professor had a chance to speak though, Arty came rushing in and sat down with them.

'When I'm wrong, I say I'm wrong. I don't know how you did it, but you did,' Arty said, out of breath.

'Yes. I hope that it will not happen again,' the Professor said to Arty before turning back to Mr Parnell. 'I'll make this quick. As I suspected, the villagers are being used to open gateways between our world and – what I will simply refer to as – the other world. A world that exists beside ours.' Both Mr Parnell and Arty looked confused so the Professor explained. 'Imagine a curtain between two rooms. Sometimes sounds and moths and smoke find tiny gaps between or above the curtain or through little holes and pass from one room to the next. This is the same with the curtain between our two worlds. It is why we sometimes see ghosts and other mysterious creatures – these are things that we can see in the other world where the veil is at its thinnest. Sometimes things can even pass through. Now, someone or something is using the villagers to make temporary holes in the curtain between our two worlds and allowing the fog, the darkness and the creatures from that world into ours. I imagine that with enough holes the curtain between our two worlds will eventually tear and all manner of hideous and unimaginable terrors from their dark world will pour into ours and overrun, not just the village, but the entire country with no way to ever send them back,' the Professor explained. Arty and Mr Parnell shook their heads, not in disbelief but in awed shock. They had seen first-hand the horrors of the other world.

'However,' the Professor continued, 'We can fight back. By using a crystal and metal compound and producing a low harmonic resonance, we can disrupt the portal, closing it shut for good and saving the villagers – if we can get to them without being killed!'

'I understood very little of that, Professor,' Arty said with a serious nod. 'But it sounds like you know what you're doing, so that's good!'

'You said something or someone is behind all this. Any ideas?' Mr Parnell asked, and the Professor shook his head.

'All I know is that the manor house in the village is at the centre of all this.'

'If whatever is causing this is in that manor house, why don't you just go straight there? Finish this once and for all,' Arty asked.

'A good question, and I did consider it. However, I suspect that whatever or whoever is behind this is drawing a power from the other realm. I think it would be disastrous to attempt to tackle the centre straight way. Instead I hope to close all the portals around the manor house and free all the lost villagers. Closing all the gateways to the other world should weaken whoever is behind this.'

'Should?' Arty asked.

'I cannot be certain, of course. This is beyond even my solid understanding. But Alexander's late father and I worked on the theories behind the opening of gateways to the other world and even worked out some calculations for transferring energy and resources from their world to ours. I can make some fairly safe assumptions and hypotheses.' The others nodded in response.

'Well, we'll leave you to it,' Mr Parnell said, standing up and leaving the room after another round of handshakes with Arty close behind. As they left, Old Dan came in carrying two bowls of steaming stew and two rolls.

'Professor, I – ' Old Dan began, struggling to find the words.

'It is what you have paid me to do,' said the Professor, 'Nothing more. Let us just hope that we can save the others as well. How is Lucy doing?'

'She's very tired. But she's awake now. She's very hungry. Eating like a horse,' Old Dan said, wiping a tear from his eye. 'Her mother is with her.'

'That's great news,' Alexander said very enthusiastically. Old Dan nodded to them both and left the room. Alexander examined the stew and tried a little but it was far too hot to eat yet so he wandered over to the window whilst it cooled. The fog had completely disappeared on this side of the tavern and he could see off to the horizon the way they had come. He was even sure he could see a strip of blue sky far off in the distance and that simple, tiny streak of colour gave him hope. The area around the tavern still looked dull though. The grass was yellow and dying and the trees were bare.

'Professor,' Alexander asked. 'When the shamblemen returned to their own world, and the fog subsided, I thought the plants and trees would turn back again too.'

'What do you mean?' the Professor said, not looking up from his notes that he was adding to.

'Well, why hasn't the grass turned green again?'

'Don't be ridiculous, Alexander! This is science, not magic! Grass that has browned through lack of sunlight will not suddenly turn green because a fog has lifted. It will take days, maybe even months, for things to return as they once looked.'

'Sorry, Professor, but the line between magic and science seems to have been blurred. Walking scarecrows, moving trees, giant creatures, wouldn't you agree we must accept that magic is real now?'

'No, Alex, I would not. A thousand years ago we thought the sun rising every morning was magic. Now we understand how the Earth rotates. Just a few hundred years ago we thought rainbows were magic. Now we understand how light refracts through prisms and water. Explorers thought it was magic the first time they saw elephants and giant crocodiles and plants that eat flies. Now walking scarecrows and moving trees are magic to us until we study them better. Mysticism is merely a way to explain things we are too lazy to understand. We have chosen to call our ignorance magic because it makes us look wise instead of foolish. Do not allow yourself to be so naïve!'

'Sorry, Professor,' Alexander apologised, and thought how he could quickly change the subject. 'How does the compound work?' he asked – the first thing that popped into his head.

'It was a formula your father and I began to work on many years ago. There are certain chemicals we found that we could combine to open the very fabric that separates us from this other world. Using it in different ways we hoped we could open a small gap between worlds for a fraction of a second, or close a dangerous tear. But we could never keep a gateway open for more than a split second though. We were unable to perfect the formula. Your father sadly passed away before we could finish it, but someone has obviously found a way of using humans as a key to keep the door between our worlds open. Using a living being as a key is not something we considered.'

Alexander had not expected the conversation to turn to his late father. The Professor rarely spoke of him. 'Why were you two studying it? What did you hope to achieve?' Alexander asked, keen to learn more whilst the Professor was talkative.

'We were studying areas of the country where the wall between our worlds might be weakest. It seemed the most haunted and troubled places in the country had the weakest partition between our world and the other. That was no surprise to us. We found a little town in Cornwall that lies on the north coast not far from Tintagel – a place steeped in strange sightings. It was remote enough that we could be left alone to our studies, but had also had numerous reports of ghosts and shadows, shipwrecks and other strange sightings so that we could assume the wall between worlds was weak there.'

'Was that the last time you saw my father – in Cornwall?' Alexander asked, trying to sound nonchalant.

'It was. I do not tend to think back to those months in Cornwall before your father died. He was very different to the man I became friends with all those years before. I suppose you are old enough to know the truth now, Alexander. But it might not be easy to hear. Mark, your father, was always passionate, incredibly bright and inventive – a genius really. However, towards the end, his passion overcame him. He became obsessed with finding a way to this other world. The knowledge and answers that lay just on the other side of the thin veil between our worlds took up his every waking hour. He stopped sleeping, barely ate and began to take foolish risks – with his own life and the lives of other people too.'

The Professor stood up and walked to the window, gazing out at the browned grass around them.

'We were running low on resources and funding. I travelled back to Cambridge to see if I could find new sponsors. I suppose in many ways I was almost as obsessed as him. I suggested stopping our studies once, but your father turned on me. He was going to continue with or without my help so I made the decision that he would be safer if we continued together. Mark refused to return with me to Cambridge to raise more funds and stayed on in Cornwall. That was probably the last straw for your poor mother too. You were just ten years old and she had to cope on her own. She was fed up with his broken promises to return as the greatest scientist of our age, the first explorer in another world. Your mother did not want that. She just wanted the man she married to come back. But your father would have seen that as a failure.' The Professor paused for a second to look at Alexander and sighed.

'Please, continue Professor. I want to know.'

'Alright,' he said, and looked back out of the window beyond the horizon. 'Your mother moved out of the family home but became very unwell some weeks later. Mark was still saying he was too close to finding a way to the other world to come back. Too close to stop and come back to Cambridge. A month or so later when I returned to Cornwall there was a boy waiting for me with a letter. It was from one of the villagers I had grown to know. The letter said that there had been a large flash of light from our makeshift laboratory and a fire had broken out. A few locals tried to put the blaze out, but it burned through the night. When they searched the burnt-out wreckage of our laboratory in the morning, nothing was left. Both your father and the housemaid I had left to ensure he ate at least once a day were never found.' The Professor turned back to Alexander who sat silently on the edge of his bed. 'I am sorry, Alexander.'

'Could he have survived?' Alexander asked.

'As hard as it is to accept the truth, you must know that he surely perished in that fire, along with the housekeeper and all our work. Goodness knows what he was working on at the end.'

Alexander nodded and thought on all this for some time. He never imagined his father to be a hero. His late grandparents had told him enough stories for him to know that his father was at best a flawed and troubled genius. Slowly, Alexander's thoughts returned to their present situation and he decided he was too hungry to think about anything very hard. He sat down and began to eat his stew. He was halfway through a mouthful when he heard the door open and someone come up behind him and plant a kiss on his cheek. Alexander looked around and saw Lucy, her big, green eyes staring down at him and her red hair swept behind her shoulders. Alexander smiled and went to say something but then half dribbled, half coughed the stew that was in his mouth all down himself. She laughed. Not a mocking laugh, or an embarrassed laugh, just a happy to be alive again laugh. Alexander smiled back, his cheeks burning scarlet, as he wiped himself down.

'If I could speak to you later please, Lucy. I have a few questions for you – only if you feel up to it, of course,' the Professor asked.

'My dad said you probably would do. Not right now though, if that's alright. Maybe later.'

'Of course.'

'Glad to see you're well,' Alexander said, regretting how stupid that must have sounded as soon as he'd said it but she smiled all the same.

'Well, only thanks to you and the Professor. If it wasn't for you two I'd still be ... ' she paused for a moment, her smile fading away and her eyes moving off to some remembered hell. ' ... wherever I was. So thank you', and with that, she walked back out of the room. Old Dan glared at him from the doorway and Alexander quickly looked away, his smile vanishing.

'Smoothly done,' the Professor said, looking up from his ledger, a hint of a smile on his lips.

5

The Lake

AFTER THEY HAD FINISHED THEIR SUPPER Alexander was hoping to lie down for a while or at least be able to check and make sure that Lucy was still alright, however the Professor had other ideas.

'I want to head out again before nightfall. I'm afraid that if whoever is in that manor house knows we are coming, they will put up a greater defence,' the Professor said, tucking his notebook inside his long, leather jacket.

'Sure. Do we have enough compound?'

'Plenty. But I do need you to make sure that your violin case is water-proof. Seal it with wax if you need to. We are heading out to the lake and there is a good chance one or both of us will end up getting very wet.'

'Lovely,' Alexander said dryly. The Professor didn't seem to notice the sarcasm though and tucked his other writing materials inside one of his many pockets and headed out of the little back room. Alexander followed him out into the main area where the atmosphere seemed more positive. People were eating and talking more eagerly and there were even smiles dotted about the room. Following the Professor upstairs he headed into his room as the Professor carried on down the corridor and up the stairs. Alexander dutifully wax sealed his violin case and put on a woollen top which Arty came in to lend him. Sighing, he looked out of the window towards the village – he really didn't want to be back in a pond again.

When he had double checked his pack, he met the Professor downstairs and they both headed out. This time the villagers seemed genuinely worried for them.

'Good luck!' and 'Come back safe!' they cried out as the Professor and Alexander left the warm security of the tavern. Outside it was cool and growing darker. There was a sweetness to the air though, pollen or the smell of crops drifting in from miles away, giving Alexander hope, and covering the damp, rotting smell that had pervaded the village.

The walk started off almost pleasantly down the gravel track, and past the fields, but slowly, as they drew closer to the village, the mist began to thicken until they were back in the fog. Alexander wrapped his arms around himself as the temperature dropped. It wasn't cold enough for ice to form, but he didn't think it could be far off. The track sloped down and all the while the fog thickened and the temperature plummeted until they reached the bank of a lake. The lake was certainly far larger than the pond he had fallen into on his arrival. A thin mist covered the opposite bank, hiding the lake's true size but the silhouette of a boat house could just be seen not too far off to his right. They walked a little further around the lake towards the boathouse and then there it was. A doorway to the other world appeared only visible when viewed from where they stood. It was totally invisible from the back or the side but appeared when viewed face on. Through the portal, in that other world, he saw a great, bubbling marshland with a colossal creature walking away from where he stood. The creature's six legs, or tentacles may have been more accurate, stepped over fog-wreathed trees before it sank down into the marshes.

'It's incredible, Professor,' Alexander said, unable to tear his eyes away from the terrible beauty of the other world.

'That it is,' the Professor agreed, putting a hand on Alexander's shoulder and nodding as he too stared transfixed at the gateway. 'I worked for so long with your father to try to produce a stable portal. We never considered the consequences. Not then anyway.' Alexander didn't say anything in reply. He knew the Professor was talking more to himself than to him anyway.

Beneath and in front of the portal stood a marble statue of a woman in the middle of the lake, half in this world, half swallowed up by that other place. The statue had presumably once been an impressive fountain of glistening marble with clear, flowing water, but now the statue was a dull grey and only dark slime hung from the vase the figure held. Moss and grime covered half of the statue's face and the trough she stood in.

The water was perfectly still, like a mirror that had not been cleaned for a very long time. It was only broken by an abandoned rowing boat that drifted aimlessly across the water, hardly making a ripple. Nothing else moved. There was no sound and the stillness was terrifying.

'Look! There in the middle,' Alexander said through chattering teeth, pointing a shivering finger to the fountain in the middle of the lake. Laying half hidden in the fountain trough was the ghost of a boy almost lost to sight against the grey stone.

There was a splash that made Alexander jump and cry out. Large ripples spread out from the water to the side of the fountain.

'That sounded big,' he said. The Professor ignored him, studying the ripples as they spread out across the water.

Alexander wanted to step back but followed the Professor who was edging closer to the lake, the ground turning to mud beneath their feet, squelching and covering their boots.

More ripples now spread out from the lake, smaller this time, and he saw a writhing, wriggling mass below the film that covered the water. Breaking the surface, a black tangle was spinning and rolling over itself. They looked like eels – fat-headed black eels fighting over something, and then, with a sinking feeling, Alexander realised they weren't eels. They were tadpoles. Giant tadpoles the length of his arm with heads larger than his fist.

'Get back from the water!' the Professor shouted. Alexander turned to run, but his feet were stuck in the mud. With a great effort he pulled one leg free with a squelch and took a step further away from the lake, but his other boot remained trapped. He turned back to the lake. The tadpoles disappeared scattering in all directions as something much larger, like a log or upturned boat, approached the shore.

The something rose further out of the water and exposed more of itself as it came into the shallows. First, two yellow eyes appeared, then a dark-green, bulbous head and then finally its repulsive, obese body. It was a frog – a huge frog, larger than any carriage or animal he had ever seen before. It could have quite easily fitted a fully grown cow into its mouth and had room for more and it was now staring at Alexander with dead, glassy eyes.

It shuffled further out of the water on podgy legs, opening its cavernous mouth to lick the air with a black, snake-like tongue.

'Alex, the row-boat! Get to the boy and use the compound. I will try to get you some time!' the Professor yelled, throwing Alexander the compound. Alexander caught it and held it tightly in his fist whilst the Professor went striding back up the muddy embankment.

Alexander abandoned his boot, pulling his leg free and scrambled away from the frog as it paused to choose which of them to pursue. Slipping and sliding around the water's edge, Alexander headed to where the row boat was bobbing near a reed-bed full of browning, wilting plants. He had only taken a few steps into the icy water when the giant tadpoles darted towards him and writhed around his feet. He sploshed back onto the mud panting in terrified high-pitched wheezes. 'Hurry!' a cry came from across the lake. The frog was moving at a speed that shocked Alexander. It crawled quickly up the bank towards the Professor, its black tongue lolling from one side of its giant mouth.

Alexander swore under his breath and waded in again. Immediately the tadpoles swarmed in again, chewing and pulling at his bootless foot. Dropping down as the lake deepened, the water rose to his waist and Alexander gasped at the cold. He dived forward to try to swim the last few yards towards the wooden rowboat. The water felt like ice, and his body went numb, a flash of pain searing across his skull. His pack and his violin case were dragging him down but it was the mass of tadpoles that terrified him. They twisted and thrashed around him, taking small bites out of his clothes. One bit at his finger and he yelped out in pain taking in a mouthful of stagnant water as he did so. Another tadpole bit his cheek and another was wriggling against his flailing arms to try to get to his neck. The stings of their teeth were all over him.

He threw a numb and shaking hand out and grabbed the prow of the boat. It bobbed and moved away but he hauled it back. Blood from the gash on his hand mixed with the water, and red streaked down his arm like lightning. Dropping the jar of compound into the boat he grabbed on with both hands and tried to pull himself up. His clothes and pack were soaked through and made his legs feel like lead and still the huge tadpoles, tumbled over each other in a feeding frenzy, dragging him down, taking tiny chunks out of his skin. Alexander felt himself being pulled back by the writhing mass and knew that if he fell backwards he would not be getting back out. He cried out and pulled with all his strength, managing to swing one leg over the side of the boat. Tumbling in, he hit his head on the side and he lay on the bottom of the boat panting, the sound of thrashing all around him. The boat rocked and banged with the cloud of tadpoles knocking against its side trying to get to him. Putting his arms on either side of him, he pulled himself up. His trousers were now nothing but rags, torn to shreds to reveal hundreds of tiny bites. The rain water in the boat had already turned a crimson colour and the world around him darkened and grew silent as his vision clouded over.

'Alex! Hurry!' a voice bellowed from across the water. It was enough to bring Alexander back into the moment, a fresh wave of adrenaline coursing through him. One broken oar lay beside him. He picked it up and began to use it like a canoe paddle, struggling to feel his hands through the cold. Managing to manoeuvre the boat closer towards the fountain he stared in at that other domain. He could feel the paddle striking against the tadpoles' bodies as he moved it through the dark water but he could focus on nothing but this view into the other world, a place so different from his own. He paddled right up beside the statue and stepped into the fountain trough, picking up the jar of compound as he did so. Being just a few feet away from that other world made him dizzy, like he was staring down from the top of a cliff at the abyss below. Stale mists blew in from that place, pouring over the boy that lay at his feet. To look at him was to stare at a ghost. He was there, sometimes clear, solid and with colour, other times he was almost totally translucent, like a picture of a boy painted on smoke.

Reaching behind him, he swung the violin case off his back and opened it up on his knees, breaking the wax seal that he had made. The violin was damp but playable, the wax join had protected it extraordinarily well. Uncorking the bottle of compound, he poured some into his hand then threw it into the air over the ghost as he had seen the Professor do. He then took his violin and rested it under his chin with his left hand, taking the bow in his right. Raising his right elbow high, he pressed down hard on the strings dragging the bow across them. The note was off. His hands were too cold and numb and he couldn't stop shaking. He shook out his hands, repositioned his fingers and tried again. This time the note was a solid G and the air shimmered like a heat haze all around him, the particles of compound vibrating in reaction to the violin. Alexander kept the note going, moving the bow back and forward and never taking his eyes off the boy. Everything seemed to hum and resonate – and then it was gone with a snap. The portal and the other world vanished but the ghost of the boy in front of him was suddenly opaque and solid. Alexander dropped the violin and pulled the boy into a sitting position.

'I've got him!' Alexander shouted over to the Professor who was lying on his back on the far side of the lake, the frog over him. The giant amphibian opened its mouth ready to swallow the Professor whole, when it disappeared. Not instantly, but fading slowly, almost melting away like a snowflake out of season. The Professor struggled to his feet where he lent on his knees and stood panting for a while before he jogged over to the shoreline closest to Alexander.

'Good work, Alex. A few seconds later and I would be digesting in that great lump's stomach. Can you get the boy into the boat safely and row back?' the Professor asked, and Alexander nodded. He guessed the tadpoles had disappeared along with the frog but he wasn't keen to find out. Slipping his hands under the boy he lowered him carefully into the boat. Once the boy was safely in, Alexander placed his violin back in its case after wiping it down and drying it as best he could. He pocketed the compound and lowered himself into the boat too. Using the oar as a punt to push the boat back to shallow water, he had a chance to look at his wounds. He wasn't in good shape. The Professor waded in once the boat hit the reeds and he scooped the boy up as if he was weightless and carried him to the bank where he laid him down. Alexander jumped out and hurried out of the lake, not wanting to ever go swimming again if he could help it.

'Do you remember what the boy's name was?' Alexander asked, staring at his pale, still face.

'Bobby Quinn,' the Professor replied. Of course he remembered, Alexander thought. 'He was the second to go missing after Lord Bleakhope's son Edgar by all accounts. We should get him back to the tavern. Hopefully he will make the same rapid recovery as Lucy when we get him warm and he has had a good rest.'

Just like before, Alexander struggled to keep pace with the Professor who strode on up the hill with Bobby over his shoulder. More of the mist had dissipated now and the sky above this side of the village was not the low and heavy grey it had been before, but a lighter grey, almost white and the cloud cover seemed to be much higher up. By the time they reached the tavern it felt warm and Alexander had almost dried out. He ran ahead of the Professor and opened the door for him. As soon as they stepped inside a woman came running up to them sobbing. She grabbed Bobby from the Professor's arms and swept him away. Another man, presumably Bobby's father, grabbed the Professor in a bear hug and squeezed him. The Professor didn't return the man's embrace and Alexander wasn't even sure if the Professor knew how to react. He'd never seen the Professor hug someone or show affection. The Professor simply nodded back without a smile and shook Mr Quinn's hand.

Alexander enjoyed some hearty congratulations of his own with the villagers fussing over his wounds and fetching him dry clothes. Before he had a chance to put on any of the new clothes the Professor made Alexander heat some water and take a bath, not only to warm him up properly but, more importantly, to tend to his many cuts and gouges. If any of them became infected, he could die within days. Alexander did as he was told and heated up some water over the fire in one of the back rooms until he had half-filled a bath tub. He poured in a generous amount of a brown liquid the Professor had given him. Professor Cordite had told him that it would sting worse than when he was being bitten but that it would be good for him and kill off any infection.

He almost jumped out of the bath as the disinfectant found every tiny graze on his body. Alexander could feel every bite all over him as if they were on fire, but the pain soon faded and, just as the water was getting cold, he began to feel relaxed. Stepping out onto the cold stone tiles he dried himself, got dressed into the clean clothes and took off with every intention of going to bed. As he passed through the tavern towards the stairs the villagers smiled and nodded at him.

'Alexander!' a voice called out from somewhere in the gloom of one of the tavern corners. Alexander looked around and saw Arty leaning forward from a chair by the entrance. 'Can you get a tune out of that violin of yours, or is it just for closing doors to other worlds?' Arty said with a smile.

'I know the odd tune. You want to hear one?' Alexander said, already taking his violin case off his shoulder. He never needed an excuse to play to a captive audience, and they didn't come much more captive than here.

'We haven't had music in this tavern for well over a year. It would be good to hear something,' Old Dan said, sitting himself down ready to listen. There was a general bustling about the room as other people came over to his side of the tavern near the big fireplace to sit down. Unclipping the three catches on the case, Alexander took out the violin and plucked the strings, adjusting the tuning pegs when the note was not as crisp as he would have liked. The room was suddenly silent.

He started off by playing a rousing version of *Married to a Mermaid*, which was always a popular one. It required some fast finger work and he could tell that people were enjoying it, even a few of them joined in on the chorus. He then followed that up with *Heart of Oak*, which was a far simpler tune, but he knew everyone would know the words and, sure enough, by the time the chorus came around the third time, everyone was singing and clinking tankards together. He caught Lucy staring at him from beside Old Dan, beaming from ear to ear and he almost lost his place in the song having to play the bridge section twice. By the time he finished *The Knight and the Shepherd's Daughter* for the second time everyone was up dancing and Lucy was twirling, fleet-of-foot in front of him with her father.

Alexander finished to rapturous applause and packed away his violin, much to the disappointment of his audience, but he knew the Professor would not be letting him lie in in the morning.

'That was beautiful,' Lucy said, leaning in and kissing his cheek.

Alexander felt himself blush and thought about trying to say something romantic about her being more beautiful but everything that popped into his head sounded terrible so he just stared at her for a while with a gormless smile and scarlet cheeks until he could say 'Thank you.' Old Dan quickly swooped in to save Lucy and him any further embarrassment and escorted her upstairs.

'That was wonderful, boy,' Mr Parnell said, shaking Alexander's hand with that firm grip. 'You don't know what it means to me, to all of us, to see the people here laugh and smile again. You've got a regular spot playing here if you want it when all this is over', and that got Alexander thinking of the work still left to be done.

'That's very kind of you,' Alexander said, and gathered up his possessions. 'I should head to bed now. Another busy day tomorrow I expect. Goodnight,' he said to Mr Parnell. 'Goodnight,' he called out to the grinning villagers.

'Goodnight,' they called back and 'Night boy'. Alexander smiled and floated upstairs.

He opened the door to his room and tiptoed inside. Two other villagers were getting into the other beds and preparing for sleep. Alexander knew he was supposed to check the supplies but he was giddy and too tired. He could do it in the morning, he thought, and his head had barely touched the pillow before he was asleep.

It seemed he had only closed his eyes for a few minutes when he awoke to the Professor shaking him.

'Time to get up and dressed. We are off to the mill!'

6

The Mill

ALEXANDER GOT HIMSELF READY, CHECKED HIS violin and repacked his bag. Old Dan threw him a roll, for which Alexander nodded his thanks, and stepped outside. Sunlight was shining down onto the tavern, only for a brief moment until the clouds blew over, but it was there and it made Alexander happier than he could have imagined. Now the thought of heading back into the cold and fog was even less appealing.

The Professor was waiting next to a cart with Arty and Nathan.

'Good, you're here,' the Professor said, as Alexander approached. 'I want to try to visit the mill and then quickly see if we can clear part of the village. As we waste a lot of time bringing the villagers back to the tavern, Arty and Nathan will join us. I also suspect that we may need more help distracting our foes as we get closer to the village.' Alexander nodded and smiled. He should have been pleased that they were going with reinforcements, but he couldn't help but feel put out that it would no longer be just the Professor and him.

'Gentlemen, are you ready?'

'Aye,' they said in unison, absentmindedly raising their weapons. Nathan carried a pitchfork and Arty a blacksmith's hammer. Arty saw Alexander stare at the hammer for a moment.

'I haven't had many horseshoes to make of late – what with there being no horses, so I thought I'd take it out and make use of it,' Arty said, with a forced smile.

'What exactly is at the mill, Professor? What are you all not telling me?' Alexander asked.

'We are just being prepared. There are rumours that there is something rather dangerous there,' the Professor said, looking away in the general direction of the mill. 'Right, enough dallying. Lead on, gentlemen.'

Once they had crossed the field and the orchard, now looking relatively peaceful, the temperature started to drop again as they entered the fog.

The almost shaven-headed Nathan took the lead with the rather rotund Arty following him. They had walked quickly to the edge of the mist where they slowed their pace and the group drew into a tighter huddle.

'Should we light torches?' Nathan asked.

'No. It will not help us see in the fog and all it will do is mark us out to anything that might be nearby. Let us try to keep as quiet as possible too,' Professor Cordite said in hushed tones.

They found themselves travelling up a gentle slope that rose on until the windmill appeared out of the fog, looming ominously over them. They slowed their pace even further as they approached and Alexander gasped and put his hand over his mouth. Thousands of threads of silver connected the windmill's sails to each other, each thread as thick as his finger. A crow struggled in the mess of threads unable to free itself. The more it struggled, the worse it became stuck. From out of the blackness of the mill's top window two massive black legs felt their way out, tapping on the wall and the threads, sensing the struggle of the bird. Then two more legs came out, long, black insect-like legs each at least as long as Alexander's own body. Then the whole creature emerged, still shaded in mist. Alexander didn't count how many legs – ten? Maybe a dozen? He was too stunned to move, fear nailing him to the spot. The creature had a segmented body, three parts, maybe four – again, he was too shocked to think anything other than that a creature like this should not exist. It was hard to tell in the fog, but it looked jet black and it scuttled effortlessly out onto the windmill's sails and ripped the trapped bird free with its pinchers and swallowed the bird whole before repairing its web and scurrying back inside.

'At least we tried,' Arty said, turning and walking away. Nathan grabbed him.

'One of the villagers is in there. It could be a child, terrified and trapped and you want to run back?' Nathan growled. Arty reluctantly turned around to face the windmill again.

'Well, I'm not going in first,' Arty huffed.

'Can we light candles now?' Nathan asked, 'It'll soon know we're here.'

'I am afraid not. We are doing this one in the dark,' said the Professor.

'I'm chuffing not!' Arty said, his hands on his hips.

'The mill could well still have bags of flour inside, torn bags of flour. Flour everywhere,' the Professor explained.

'So?'

'Any naked flame could cause a dust explosion. If a cloud of flour is ignited it will blow this whole building apart.'

'That doesn't sound like such a bad idea to me,' Arty snorted.

'I am here to save the village and the villagers, not blow them all up. No naked flames!' the Professor said, and Arty huffed again.

Alexander had never seen the Professor nervous, but he paused for a long while by the door to the windmill. 'Nathan, you open the door and I will go inside,' the Professor said, pulling his tricorn hat down tightly on his head and loading his crossbow with a large, iron bolt. Nathan nodded and stood to one side of the door reaching across it to grip the handle. He stared up at the Professor and waited for a signal. The Professor took a deep breath and nodded. Nathan yanked open the door so hard it nearly tore off its hinges. Raising his crossbow, the Professor scanned the darkness inside. Nothing but the stench of decay and a cloud of dust rolled out to greet them. The Professor took a step forward into the gloom and Nathan and Alexander followed him inside with Arty shuffling hesitantly in last. It took a few seconds for their eyes to become accustomed to the dark. They stared up the zig-zagging staircase that rose to the top of the mill. The mill was circular, like the inside of a tube, and there were two wooden platforms above them covering one half of the mill. It meant that they could look all the way to the top. Grey mist poured down from high above them, rolling over the side of the top platform and down over idle cogs and wheels.

'Where is it?' Nathan whispered. There were not many places for such a huge creature to lay unseen. A few crates were stacked about and bags of flour piled up, but not enough for it to hide behind.

Suddenly, movement made Alexander look up. The creature was clinging to the wall just above him. Looking like an elongated spider, it clung to the wall and silently moved down towards them. Alexander ran forward and dived at Arty's waist, knocking the big man to the ground just as the creature's giant pincers snapped at the air where Arty's head had been just a split second before. Alexander rolled onto his knees and scrambled to one side of the mill fearful it would come for him next. He heard the thud and twang of the crossbow being fired and the creature let out a high-pitched cry and scuttled higher up the wall to the top of the mill and onto the top floor out of sight.

'Did you hit it?' Alexander asked.

'I did, not fatally though,' Professor Cordite said, reloading an iron bolt. 'Nathan, stay here. Arty, you wait on the first floor. Alex and I will go to the top floor and we will try to finish it. If it comes back down try to distract it.' The men nodded. 'Alex, get your violin ready.' Alex did as he was told, taking his violin out of its case. The Professor led the way up the first flight of steps to the lowest platform. Huge gears and rusting poles lay about the platform. They heard a scuttling noise on the floorboards above. 'If there is a portal here, it must be on the top floor!' the Professor whispered.

Threads of webbing crisscrossed the walls of the top of the mill and some strange, half-eaten animal was encased in sticky gossamer. Thankfully, whatever the animal had been, Alexander was certain it wasn't human. He was pretty sure it wasn't even of this world. They crept onto the first floor platform and looked over the edge to Nathan who paced nervously about on the ground floor looking around him, his pitchfork held out ready.

'Arty, wait here. Alex and I will continue up,' the Professor said, and Arty nodded, taking his position in the centre of the platform, his hammer gripped tightly in two shaking hands. Leading the way again, the Professor made his way slowly up the final set of steps, checking every possible angle where the creature could attack from. 'It looks clear of the beast, but there is a portal here,' he said, after peeking around. They carefully made their way up onto the top platform. There were boxes and sacks strewn around and all the edges of the room were thick with cobwebs, but there was nowhere the giant creature could hide.

'It must have gone back outside,' Alexander said, pointing to the large window that looked out above the centre of the windmill's sails. From one corner of the room, behind a mass of grey threads, he could see the ghostly luminescence of the portal, a view into the other world. Strange, jagged rock formations, dark as the night, rose up out of the mist and twisted back on themselves, like waves. Webs had been spun between the huge rocks and in the distance there was a tower – a massive, dark stone tower stretching off into the sky, lit from within by torch light.

Alexander ran over and the Professor took a knife out of his belt and began to cut away at the web revealing more of the portal. Deep within the webbing, glowing from beneath the filth, was a women dressed in a simple, white dress. For a moment she looked as if she was sleeping until she began to fade and reappear like Lucy and Bobby had done – a ghost between worlds. The Professor took out a container and poured some of the compound into his hand.

Launching itself forward from the darkness of the window, the spider-like creature shot inside and knocked the Professor over the edge of the platform sending a cloud of the compound into the air.

'Professor!' Alexander screamed, as he ran to the edge after him. The Professor was holding onto the ledge with one hand, his whole body dangling thirty feet in the air. If the fall didn't kill him Alexander knew it would leave him with two broken legs. Surveying its prey, the creature moved about the ceiling above them, its sharp legs tapping the ceiling, its mandibles and pincers snapping aggressively. Alexander held the violin and bow in one hand and reached out with the other for the Professor to take. 'Grab on!'

'Your violin! Play! Just play!' the Professor shouted back, managing to get his other hand onto the side of the platform. Alexander jumped back as the creature moved towards him and paused at the edge of the platform where the Professor was dangling. Drool dripped down onto the Professor's hands. Alexander got his fingers set and played the note. The creature swung itself around to face Alexander. It cried out, scuttling back onto the ceiling and then back down the wall to drop in front of Alexander again – the vibrations the violin was creating seeming to violently agitate it.

Alexander backed himself against the wall, the sticky threads that dangled there clinging to him. The creature moved closer, its pincers stretching wide, more drool dripping from its gaping, dark mouth. Alexander stopped playing and tried to run, but he was stuck, caught in its web. The creature coiled itself up ready to strike and then sprang at Alexander certain to bite him clean in two. From Alexander's right, a huge hammer came flying across the room and struck the creature in the head sending it reeling back, its black legs twitching and flicking around. Arty charged over and stood between the creature and Alexander. Alexander didn't hesitate. He played the note again, struggling to move with his arm sticking to the web. The vibrations returned and every atom in the mill started shaking. For a second, the other world flickered and then it was gone with a snap and a gust of wind. The twitching creature faded like a dream upon waking. Nathan shot up to the top of the steps and ran to the Professor, hauling him back onto the platform.

They all stood there panting for a few seconds. Arty glanced over to Alexander and looked as though he was going to say something, but he simply nodded to him. Alexander wanted to thank him for returning the favour and saving his life, but words seemed so hollow after what had happened so he simply nodded back.

'Sarah!' Nathan shouted, and pushed between them to get to the woman dressed in white. 'It's my Sarah! Is she alright,

Professor?' The Professor stood up straight and went to check on her. He felt her forehead and saw her breathing.

'She will be fine if she recovers like the other two,' the Professor said, nodding and still breathing hard. 'You should get her back, Nathan. Arty, Alex and I can continue to the village.'

'Thank you, Professor,' Nathan said, crying and hugging her limp body.

'It is what you paid us for. Nothing more.'

Arty went to help him carry his wife down the stairs, but Nathan really didn't need it. He could have carried Arty too and not struggled. Once the Professor had helped cut Alexander out of the cobweb, they made their way down the stairs too and Alexander packed his violin away, putting it over his shoulder. Outside, in the emerging sunlight, Nathan headed back off towards the tavern with Sarah over his shoulder, his pitchfork left discarded on the floor.

'I better take that for him,' Alexander said, picking it up and feeling immediately braver now he was carrying something slightly more deadly than a violin. 'Professor, what did we see back there through the portal?'

'It is going to take me a while to process and think it through. I am not even certain of what I saw. It all happened so quickly.'

'But it was a building we saw, wasn't it? There was a tower! The other world isn't just some wild, untamed land. There are buildings there!' Alexander said, confused, frightened and excited at the same time. 'What does that mean?'

'It means that there is some form of intelligent life in that other world. They must have builders and architects. Perhaps they look like us. Perhaps not. But I fear we will know more before this mission is over.' He turned and raised his voice. 'Arty, are you happy to continue towards the village?' Arty shrugged and then nodded sombrely in reply.

They had only walked for ten minutes, though, when they saw that they were not going to be able to get to the village. Bushes of thorns surrounded the village like a citadel wall. Alexander guessed the wall of barbed creepers was at least ten feet tall and maybe as thick. They split into two groups, Alexander and the Professor heading one way, and Arty the other. They walked around the spiky wall to look for an opening or way in for ten minutes before Alexander saw movement in the thorn bush. They slowed down and crept closer to see what it was. For a second Alexander could see a rabbit with thorny vines snaked around its body, then the bush seemed to drag the rabbit further into the darkness and the movement stopped. They trudged back and met Arty where they had started.

'Any luck?' Arty asked.

'No. This wall seems to go all the way around the village,' the Professor said, hands on hips, surveying the scene.

'It wasn't here last week,' Arty said in wonder. 'It's just not possible!'

'I suspect that this only appeared after they became aware of us rescuing two of the villagers. It probably appeared last night,' the Professor said, stepping closer and inspecting the thorns that were each as long as a finger. He cut through a chunk of the vines with his knife and then hacked away at the thicker branches, careful not to be caught by the deadly looking thorns. They cut cleanly, but the severed vines writhed around on the floor like worms before moving, caterpillar-like, back into the bush. New vines stretched forward and rebuilt the tear that the Professor had made.

'Well, we're not hacking our way through,' Arty said, shaking his head.

'Could we burn it?' Alexander asked.

'Possibly, but I think it would regenerate too fast,' the Professor said, and paused for a long time whilst they all thought of a plan. 'Let us return to the tavern to think,' he said after a while. No one argued.

They walked back to the tavern in silence, the Professor clearly thinking of a plan. Alexander was trying to think of a way past the thorns too – ladders over the top? Digging a tunnel? But for every idea he came up with, he'd think of ten good reasons why it wouldn't work.

Back in the tavern the mood was upbeat and Nathan was telling the story of the rescue. Sarah was already sitting down with him, a healthy glow to her cheeks.

'Mr Parnell, a word please,' the Professor said and Arty and Alexander followed the two men into the back room.

The Professor explained to Mr Parnell what had happened and about the impenetrable wall of thorns.

'I just do not see how we can get through, not without an army,' the Professor said, slumping back in his chair and rubbing his forehead. Alexander could not remember ever seeing the Professor so crestfallen.

'Then there's no way to get to the village now? It's over!' Arty said.

'There is one way. I would tell you how dangerous it is, but I know you won't listen,' Mr Parnell said.

'What way is that?' the Professor asked, sitting up straight.

'There is an old tunnel that runs from the church in the village to this tavern. It was built when the King was hunting down every priest in England. It's an escape tunnel of sorts. You can reach it from the cellar here.'

'Why were we not told of this before?' the Professor asked, slightly annoyed.

'Firstly, you never asked. But more importantly is the fact that no one has used it in years,' Mr Parnell said, shaking his head and resting back in his seat. 'I remember my grandfather telling me stories about the tunnel and he never knew anyone who had gone through it, not for sure. It's almost a quarter of a mile long, it's pitch black and could well be blocked up and caved-in in places. We actually did try to use it a few months back, to see if the village was still accessible this way, but something's down there now. Something big – something terrible.'

7

The Tunnel

'GOOD. WE LEAVE IN TEN MINUTES. Alex, bring torches, lamps and spare flint. Also, find a spade!' the Professor said as he stood and straightened out his hat before heading up to his room. Arty and Mr Parnell just stared at Alexander.

'Oh good,' Alexander said.

'I'll give you a hand,' Arty said, and left the room. Alexander stayed where he was in the back room and checked that his violin was tuned correctly, tweaking the tuning pegs until he was satisfied.

Arty returned with two lamps and a shovel. 'There you go.'

'Are you coming with us?' Alexander asked.

'Not this one. The Professor just told me and Nathan it would be too cramped in the tunnel with so many of us. Something about tripping each other over and not putting anyone's life at risk unless he had to,' Arty said, probably secretly relieved he wasn't going. 'But you come back in one piece, alright?' he added, slapping an arm on Alexander's shoulder.

'I'll try to,' Alexander said, smiling back, and he set off to his room to grab his spare flints and matches. After feeling put out with Arty and Nathan joining him that morning, he now found he very much wanted them alongside him.

Once Alexander had sorted everything they needed, he went back downstairs to meet the Professor. Old Dan led them through the back corridors, and down several short flights of steps. They came to a bare storeroom where Old Dan had to light several lamps on each wall to allow them to see anything.

'Just last year this room was filled with barrels of ale and salted meat. Pheasants and turkeys hung from the rafters and rabbits from the walls. Now look at it,' Old Dan said, hands on his hips, shaking his head. Alexander looked around at the pitiful sight. All the hooks on the walls were empty and no barrels remained. A few boxes littered the floor, but Alexander doubted they contained much. In the corner of the room, though, was a flight of stairs leading down into darkness. Alexander followed the two men to the top of the stairs and gazed down into the black. If it were just him, Alexander would have stood there all day just staring, not daring to move, but the Professor, lamp in hand, just strode on down the stairs as if he didn't have a care in the world. Old Dan went next and Alexander quickly followed, not wanting to be left alone in any of these rooms.

Descending into the lower cellar Alexander shivered as the air grew damp, cold and heavy. It was tainted with a mouldy, animal smell. Beneath his feet were shallow puddles on the bare bricks. The room looked to be a dead end – the bare earth walls had nothing on them, there were no doors or further stairs. There were just three large crates and two barrels squeezed in one corner.

'Give me a hand,' Old Dan said, walking over to the barrels. He took hold of one of them by wrapping his arms around it and dragged it to the ground. The Professor joined him and hauled the other barrel off. Together they moved the barrels and the three boxes, pulling them one at a time into the other corner. As they did, they revealed a wooden trapdoor.

'This is it,' said Old Dan. 'And this is where I leave you, I'm afraid. Good luck, gentlemen. We all wish you both a safe return.' Old Dan forced a smile and left the room, walking quickly back up the stairs. It was just the Professor and Alexander again.

'Stand back. I'm going to open the door,' the Professor said, putting his lamp carefully down, spitting on his hands and taking hold of the large iron ring. He gripped it with both hands and pulled. Plumes of dust swirled around as he heaved the trapdoor open and carefully lowered it to the floor so as not to make too much noise. A foul stench rose up from the darkness and the Professor crouched next to the trapdoor and lowered the lamp down.

'Looks clear,' he said, and began to lower himself into the tunnel, holding on to a rusty ladder that was attached to one side. Alexander took a deep breath, put the handle of the lamp in his mouth and climbed down beside him, looking back up to watch the square of light above him slowly shrink. Once at the bottom of the ladder he dropped down onto cracked stone tiles. Either side of him were more bare earth walls with rocks and stones jutting out every few feet. He walked alongside the Professor and they began to head forward into the tunnel at a brisk pace with only the area directly around them visible in their lamplight.

It was a tight squeeze to stand next to the Professor and it was far easier to walk one behind the other. Alexander had no desire to be leading the way, but he didn't want to be at the back either. Every forty steps or so the tunnel widened out into little alcoves where the two of them could stand side by side for a moment before the Professor took the lead again.

Simply breathing was getting harder with every step as the air grew thicker, and still the tunnel sloped downward taking them deeper underground. Just as the floor began to level out, they heard a noise in front of them. Alexander and the Professor froze, lamps held outstretched. It was a scratchy sound, like someone dragging knives across stone some distance away. It stopped as quickly as it had started and they were left in silence. They waited for a long while before the Professor took another step and froze again. There was a rustling noise now and the same quick scrape of something sharp against stone.

'We should go back,' Alexander said, involuntarily shuffling back the way they had come, one hand on the cold earth wall to steady himself, the other shaking hand holding the lamp in front of him. His trembling made the lamplight flicker and caused the shadows of the uneven wall to jump and dance around him. Then, further down the tunnel, two dull, little lights appeared. With sudden dread, Alexander realised that they weren't new lights, but his own lamplight reflected back at him – eyes. Two eyes were staring back at him, lit only by the orange lamplight. Something was still hidden in the shadows and Alexander wasn't going to wait to find out what it was. He turned to run back but a firm hand gripped his shoulder.

'Stand your ground!' the Professor growled. For a moment Alexander felt fortified but then he turned back to the glowing eyes further down the corridor and he began to tremble again. Scratch, scratch, scratch came the noise and the glowing eyes came closer. Lowering his lamp carefully to the floor, the Professor took the crossbow from off his shoulder and loaded a bolt. There was a loud screech that echoed down the narrow tunnel and Alexander dropped the lamp with a startled cry. The lamp smashed on the floor and the flame spluttered out leaving only the Professor's lamp burning. With another screech the creature darted towards them, its claws scraping on the stone floor. Only at the last second when it was a few feet away from where Alexander cowered beside the Professor did the light reveal what it was. A giant bird at least six feet tall. With the flicking light from below it made its giant form look even more ghastly. The bird was black all over and could have been an enormous crow, but its beak was longer – like that of a kingfisher. A bolt shot from the Professor's bow and the bird writhed around screeching, not able to open its wings fully in the narrow corridor. It shrieked and shook its head violently from side to side. Cawing and pecking, it lashed out at the Professor who stumbled back and clutched at a patch of red on his thigh. The bird cawed again and went to peck at Alexander but the Professor grabbed the lamp and swung it at the bird's giant head. In the flash of firelight Alexander saw its cold, dead eyes show no signs of fear or pain. Then they were in total darkness.

Alexander felt sick as the weight of the darkness pressed against him. He scurried back on all fours and curled himself up into a ball against the side of the tunnel and began to sob. A giant claw landed next to him. He couldn't see it, but he heard the scraping of talons next to him on the stones – talons ready to grab him and tear him to shreds. He could smell the creature too – mould and animal waste. Alexander wanted to run, he wanted to stay curled up, he wanted to be anywhere other than that tunnel. Covering his mouth to stop his sobbing, he heard the Professor crawling away and wincing at the injury he had sustained. Alexander wanted to call out to him, but was too afraid to speak in case it attracted the bird's attention. The claws scraped past him and still he stayed pressed against the wall hugging his knees. He heard the Professor cry out but could not tell if it was in pain or anger but the noise was enough to break Alexander's paralysis. He stood up as quietly as he could, leaning against the wall, and staggered away. Away from the bird. Away from the Professor. Away to anywhere but there.

The tunnel went on and on and still he could hear that terrible bird cawing out behind him. In front of him a light blur appeared. Alexander wasn't sure if it was real or imagined and had to wave his hand in front of his face to check. There was light, light at the end of the tunnel. Alexander quickened his pace and the light grew until he found himself in the bottom of a huge crater in the middle of a church. He could see the stained-glass windows and the pillars rising up to the rafters high above him. The sides of the crater were rubble where the tunnel entrance must have collapsed, but he couldn't work out why there was so much wood at the bottom of the hole. The wood wasn't broken timbers or rafters – the church walls and roof looked intact from what he could see from the bottom of the crater. But beneath him there were sticks and branches everywhere, they covered the floor and looked as though they had been badly woven or pulled together. Then he noticed three, large, white rocks in one corner. They stood out from the other rocks, not just because they were white against the grey of the rubble, but because they were perfectly smooth, like marble. And that was when Alexander realised where he was. It was a nest. A nest with three eggs in it.

Alexander grabbed at the rubble and scrambled out of the crater on all fours. Once he was out of the pit and safely on the church floor he could see the portal behind the altar. Through the gateway to the other world he could see a perfectly flat plateau of mist stretching as far as the horizon. A sea of mist. Above him the sky was grey but a huge, orange moon far different to his own filled half the sky. There seemed to him to be something very sacrilegious about a doorway to the other realm within the church and he wanted to close it as quickly as he could.

Lying on the floor behind the altar was a young man in his early twenties, flickering, half in the church, half in the other realm. Alexander took the compound out and threw a cloud of it into the air. Taking his violin out of its case he shouldered it and positioned the bow. Drawing out a long G, the world began to hum and glimmer. The worlds flickered and vibrated and then there was a cracking sound and he was looking at a stained-glass window where the portal had been. The villager on the floor stopped flickering and was suddenly solid and whole.

Alexander knew the villager would be alright, but the Professor might not. He searched the corners of the church and found a candle. Lighting it, he half shuffled, half slid back down into the pit.

'Professor? Professor?' he called out, with only his echo replying. Back into the tunnel he went knowing now the bird would have vanished too, but the fear still playing on his mind. Halfway down the tunnel, Alexander found the Professor's body lying perfectly still.

8

The House

IT TOOK A WHILE FOR THE Professor to regain consciousness. With some significant effort on both their parts, they managed to get the Professor standing, and moving out of the tunnel. He was limping badly and Alexander couldn't see in the candlelight how bad it was. Once they got to the bottom of the nest and it was lighter, Alexander could see what a nasty wound it was. He dressed the deep cut as best he could after cleaning it with the brown liquid the Professor had given him. Professor Cordite had to bite down on his sleeve to stop himself crying out as Alexander dabbed the disinfectant onto the deep gash. He held out his hand for the Professor to pull himself up. He got halfway up, then cried out, and sank back to the floor.

'It's no good. We'll have to turn back. I won't be able to climb out of this pit and even if I do I won't be any use in Bleakhope Manor against whatever is causing all this. We need to go back,' the Professor said, panting, his arm over his eyes.

'I can go, Professor. I can do it!'

'No. I will not let you go in there alone.'

'With all due respect, Professor. You've brought me along with you to face living scarecrows, giant tadpoles, a great big, spider thing and a subterranean bird. I hardly think now is the time to be thinking of my safety,' Alexander said, with more force than he intended. The Professor smiled and then laughed. It was a strange sound and Alexander realised it might have been the first time he had ever heard the Professor laugh.

'Stubborn. Like your father,' the Professor said, and then looked away.

'I'm pretty sure I got that from you,' Alexander replied.

'I am not certain what you will face in there, Alex. I am not sure you will be ready for it.'

'I've faced some monstrous things from that other world these past days and survived.'

'It is not the monstrous things from that world that worry me. It is the monstrous things from this world that scare me more. Alex, in the house – ' the Professor began to say and then stopped, not sure how to go on. 'You may face a battle in the Manor. Not a physical fight, but an internal conflict. I want you to be brave, Alex. Follow your heart.' He looked down at his leg and shook his head. 'I should be there with you. This is a bad idea.'

'Professor, you've taught me well. Trust me,' Alexander said. Professor Cordite smiled, and Alexander could have sworn a tear welled in the Professor's eye.

'Take more of the compound then and keep your violin safe. If you feel in danger – well, a lot of danger – a situation beyond your capability, get out. There is no shame in that.' Alexander took the compound from the Professor and nodded.

'I'll be back for you!' Alexander said, and turned away leaving the Professor in the middle of the giant bird's nest at the bottom of the pit. He scrambled up the side of the collapsed hole and walked through the church to the large vestibule without looking back and pushed the doors open. He suddenly felt very alone.

Outside, black timber houses stood shrouded in mist and total darkness. The village was silent. There was no summer here, no sunlight. It could have been late evening on a winter's day. Alexander saw his breath rise as steam to join the fog that surrounded him. A main thoroughfare stretched from the church through the village. He couldn't see very far down the road but he assumed that the main track would lead to the manor house. Stepping out of the church, he made his way slowly past the first of the timber buildings. Alexander tried to imagine the village full of bustling market stalls, horses and laughing children – he couldn't. Thankfully the road was wide enough so that he could walk down its centre and not be too close to the buildings that lay either side of him, their large, dark windows like skulls' eye sockets.

He walked past an old school building and a shiver ran down his spine as he thought he heard whispering coming from inside. He hurried his pace and saw movement from a window. Then another shadow seemed to scurry in the mist from behind one building to another. Alexander burst into a run and he sprinted ahead, shadows moving at windows and between houses all around him. The fog grew thicker until he flew between two gate posts and the path rose steadily higher ahead of him. He turned around. He had reached the other side of the village.

Everything was still now, but he didn't wait around and carried on at a steady jog up the track not wanting to see what came after him. Within moments, Bleakhope Manor loomed out of the fog in front of him. It was an ugly, square building of grey stones and narrow, rectangular windows. Gargoyles glared down at him from above the entrance, their mouths open in warning. A faint light glowed from one window above him. Someone or something was up there.

Alexander walked up the three steps to the large door and tried the handle. The door opened, but it was stiff. Putting his shoulder against the door he managed to push it open far enough so that he could squeeze through. It took a moment for his eyes to adapt to the darkness. Mist floated about inside the hallway, much thicker than it had been outside. This was as dense a fog as he had ever seen and he was soaked through in seconds. He was barely able to see his feet through the mist. Crouching down to look at the floor Alexander saw that what he had first mistaken for a moulding rug blocking the door was a carpet of fungus. Making his way forwards he found that the white fungus stretched out across the floor and the lower half of the walls. He searched around, blind in the fog, until he came to the foot of the staircase. He began to climb, stepping carefully as to not break the fungus for fear of sending plumes of spores into the air.

Taking slow, soft steps he ascended the staircase. The handrail was covered with a thin layer of fungus and where the fungus hadn't reached yet the wood looked rotten and crumbling. The mist grew slightly thinner as he climbed and it rolled down the stairs like a gentle waterfall of smoke. He could at least see a few yards in front now. Once safely on the landing he headed down the corridor in the general direction of where he thought he had seen the light from the window. The fungus was just as thick on this floor and the floorboards bowed under his steps, sagging with the damp and mould.

The doors to his left and right were wide open, a faint light coming in from outside. The room at the far end of the corridor was shut and an orange light could be seen beneath the door illuminating the mist with an eerie glow. Alexander took his violin out of its case and checked the compound was still in his pocket. He tiptoed down the corridor, trying not to disturb the fungus. There was an unsettling quiet but he could swear he could hear the fungus almost breathing. A wheezing sound that seemed to come from all around him. He came to the end of the corridor. Swallowing, he reached out a trembling hand to the ornate door-handles when he heard a voice behind that made him scream and jump around. At first, the person's long, straggly, white hair made him think it was an old woman, but then as a gap in the fog passed by he noticed the wild beard. The old man was hunched over, leaning against the wall for support. Half his body was covered in fungus. It had crusted his clothes to his skin and had climbed up to the side of his face. Patches of once fine clothes could be seen in places, but the yellowing fungus was slowly encasing him in its parasitic shell.

'Who are you?' he wheezed, looking up at Alexander with milky white eyes. 'Edgar? Edgar, my son, is that you?' With a flash of realisation Alexander saw now that this must be Lord Bleakhope. 'Edgar, I've found you!' the old man said, trying to raise a hand blindly up in Alexander's direction, but the threads of fungus dragged his arm back down. Ideas rushed through Alexander's mind. Should he be honest, should he play along? 'I heard you so many nights. Calling to me from the shadows. Calling for me from the fog. I opened so many doors to find you. I opened all the doors I could to find you.'

It was too much for Alexander. As ghastly as the old man looked, ravaged by the creeping, pale mould, he pitied him. He wanted to hate the man who had caused such destruction on the village but found no anger there. Alexander could not find it in his heart to lie to him.

'I am not your son, but I am here to find him for you,' Alexander said. Lord Bleakhope stood still for a long time and Alexander didn't know if he had heard him or gone into some catatonic state. He snapped his head back to Alexander and gave him a smile.

'Yes. Yes there is a way you can help me find him,' he said, and took a shuffling step forwards. 'You too can become a key to open a new door!' he shouted and ran towards Alexander surprisingly fast, the fungus now seeming to act as a layer of muscle propelling him on rather than as a weight to hold him back. Alexander half dived, half fell into one of the abandoned rooms and ran behind a collapsed bed he found in its centre.

'Wait!' another voice boomed from back in the corridor. A voice that Alexander didn't recognise – or did he? It was not the Professor, although it had his commanding tone. It didn't sound like the accent of the villagers. Then Alexander had a moment of clarity, as if Professor Cordite was whispering in his ear. Lord

Bleakhope could not have done all this. He had a purpose, a reason, but this must have taken advanced scientific skill and planning. This was the work of a genius not a broken madman like Lord Bleakhope. This needed a mind like – like – like the Professor's! Lord Bleakhope stopped his pursuit and stared in Alexander's direction. Could he see through those white eyes?

'Do not harm him. Bring him to me at once!' the voice demanded. 'Alexander and I have much to discuss.'

9

The Man

LORD BLEAKHOPE ESCORTED ALEXANDER BACK TO the room at the end of the corridor, the door now wide open. The room was glowing with the ghosts of the villagers – a dozen or more – their bodies there but not there, keys to keep a giant portal open. Where the back wall of the room should have been, was the main doorway to that other world – a huge hole to an alternate realm. It was the edge of a forest, but unlike any forest that Alexander had ever seen, different from any woods that surely existed in his own world. Twenty or so black roots rose out of the mist thicker than a house to merge into one massive trunk that disappeared into the grey clouds above. There was a forest of them, hundreds of trees lifted above the mist on their roots stretching into the clouds way above. From what Alexander could see each tree could have been half a mile high. Birds, with leathery, grey skin, huge wings and long beaks circled the trees – each bird was surely far larger than a horse. It was a doorway wide open between their world and his, and there, standing in front of the open portal, stood a man.

It was not the Professor, but he had a similar look, like a dashing pirate who had decided to take up science instead. He too wore a tricorn hat like the Professor, but he wore a long, pale leather coat and white leather gloves. On the desk beside him against the wall were mirrors, tubes, candles, books, scrolls and any number of crystals and strange pieces of equipment.

'That will be all, Lord Bleakhope. You may return to your room. I shall continue the search for your son,' the man said, and Lord Bleakhope turned as if sleepwalking and shuffled off back down the corridor. The man turned back to Alexander and smiled. 'Alexander? You probably don't remember me, but I remember you. You've grown up so much. I've done all this for us, Alexander. For you and your mother!' Alexander physically recoiled. It was like being hit in the stomach.

'Father?'

'Look at you. What a fine young man you've become.'

'Father?' was all Alexander could say in reply again, his mind a spinning mess.

'I have been working so hard to make you and your mother proud. Look what I have accomplished. I am a pioneer in a new world. This is the greatest discovery man has ever made!'

'My mother is dead!' Alexander said, finding courage in his anger. How dare he mention her! His father looked down at his own feet, his face whitening.

'I didn't know that. I'm sorry, Alexander. I haven't been in contact much with – with anyone.'

'I thought you were dead! We all thought you were dead. Why?'

'A regrettable need. The breakthrough in Cornwall, when I first tore a gap open between our worlds – that was the start of it. I travelled into that other realm, causing a terrible fire behind me, but the artificial portal was unstable. I could not remain there long before the doorway threatened to collapse behind me. When I returned to this world just a few minutes later I found that many weeks in our world had passed. The house we had used as a laboratory had burnt down and I heard from the villagers close by that I had died in the fire – although my body was never discovered. I found that being presumed dead allowed me to escape the watchful eye of Professor Cordite and I could continue my work uninterrupted.'

'You never thought to come back to us. To see your family again?' Alexander asked, shaking his head in disbelief.

'What? And return a failure? Not when I was so close to achieving greatness.'

'This?' Alexander said, indicating the fungus and ghostly bodies of the villagers around him. 'This is your work? Your achievement? You did this for us?'

'Don't be so narrow minded, Alexander,' his father said, looking back to him, his eyes growing wide. 'I came here with good intentions – to find the boy, I truly did. I had heard the stories of his odd disappearance and the strange things villagers were seeing in the town over the years. The veil between our worlds is so very thin here. I was constantly listening out for such stories. Just as I had expected, the boy had slipped into the other world. He acted as an accidental key – upsetting the balance between our worlds, letting things pass backwards and forwards naturally. Do you know how rare that is? As a scientist and explorer I could not just ignore such an opportunity. There is always a price to pay for every advancement in science. The boy and the other villagers here are making a noble sacrifice for such astounding strides in knowledge and exploration.'

'How can you say such things? They are human beings. Or have you spent so long in that other place you've forgotten what it's like to be human?' Alexander shouted, and his father smiled patronisingly back at him.

'You must know that it wasn't that I didn't love you or your mother. Of course I did. But I had to make a difficult decision – a choice between love and greatness. A chance to explore a new world with a multitude of new species of flora and fauna. I have already learnt so much. The science, the laws of nature in this new world will propel our understanding forward centuries! The things we can teach the world, the things we can show them!' he exclaimed, stretching his arms out grandly as if he was delivering this speech to a crowd. Then he seemed to come back to himself and shrugged, looking as if the weight of the world was on his shoulders, as if he had no other choice. Then he ramped up his enthusiasm again, but this time it was more personable, just to Alexander. 'You can be there with me! We'll be explorers of this brave, new world. And when we show everyone what we have found we will be more than just brilliant scientists. Alexander, we will be gods!'

Alexander shook his head. 'The Professor said that you had become obsessed. He was wrong.'

His father's face lit up with a smile. 'Yes!' his father grinned.

'You're not obsessed. You're mad!' Alexander finished. His father's smile dropped and a dark sneer replaced it.

'Where is the Professor now?'

'He's coming,' Alexander lied. 'Where's Edgar?'

'Edgar? – Ah, the boy who found the gap between worlds. Playing hide and seek and discovering a doorway right here in this study that only he could see. Children perceive the world differently,' he added, as if it were an interesting aside – as if he was still giving lectures in some university hall. 'Infants can see and hear things that adults can't. A thin slither, a tear in the fabric of our world that showed him a whole new realm, how could he not explore. And once he passed through, he allowed things back in. He really started all this, you know.'

'So he's still alive?'

'Yes, a resourceful boy. How he's managed to survive I don't know, but he has. You have to remember, of course, that although he has been missing for almost half a year in our world, it has only been a few weeks for him in the other world. He found his way back to the doorway once. I couldn't let him back this side, of course. His return could seal the doorway forever. I had to drive him back into that dark place.'

'You're a monster!' Alexander cried, his fists clenching at his sides, his whole body shaking. His father's eyes narrowed then relaxed. He smiled again like he had just taken off a mask and it almost looked genuine.

'I'm not angry with you, Alexander. I'm proud. You have come so far. Look at what you've accomplished on your own. Just getting here you've shown how bright you are. You're a young, handsome man now. Come with me. Utilise your considerable talents and help me finish my work.'

'Compliments thrown around like confetti are meaningless,' Alexander said, and laughed to himself.

'Pardon?' his father asked.

'It doesn't matter. It's just something the Professor said to me once.'

'Huh!' his father laughed dryly. 'He could have been a great man.'

'He is a great man!'

'Great men do not stand in the way of progress, they drive it forward! With every person we use as a key in this world I can unlock more of the other world. Our new world. I had opened up huge swathes of land to explore, but you and the Professor have put a temporary stop to that.'

'But their world is leaking into ours! You're going to destroy this village, maybe the whole country! Where does it stop? Where do you stop?'

'I just need to return to where I was. I need to put those villagers back. Turn them back into keys between our worlds. Then a few more after that maybe. Then I will have opened up enough of the other world to – '

'What?'

'There are people there. A civilisation like our own! But they are so much more powerful. I just need to let enough of their world and atmosphere leak into ours so that they can come through,' continued Alexander's father.

'Listen to yourself!'

Bells suddenly rang out from somewhere outside. Alexander ran to the window. Church bells were ringing from down in the village. The Professor, Alexander thought. He's coming. It wasn't the Professor marching up the hill towards the manor house though, or certainly not just the Professor. It looked as if everyone from the tavern was there. Flaming torches, pitchforks and sticks were being brandished by the mob whose shouts could now be heard, defiant and angry. Alexander turned to his father with a smug smile.

'They're not afraid of you anymore. They know you can be stopped.'

'It's not me they need to be afraid of,' his father said, stepping to one side. Behind him, in that other world, a figure was striding towards them. He looked close, but he kept coming and growing larger. It was at least eight or nine feet tall, but it wasn't a man. It was a shadow in white armour. Its face was blackness contained in a helmet of smooth, pale plates with dark holes where the eyes and mouth should be. Then Alexander realised it was not armour, but the creature's own skeleton. Not an internal skeleton like the bones of a mammal, but external, like a beetle or a spider. Its body was long and thin, the bone armour covering almost all of its elongated darkness. Stretched, like the shadow of a man at dusk or dawn and wreathed in a shell of ivory. Its black, hollow eyes burned into Alexander. 'Now you too will understand, my son,' his father said, stepping back further.

Alexander couldn't move. He wanted to run, or scream as this lord of shadows, this grotesque abomination walked into Alexander's own world, a fresh pool of mist spilling from the portal into the study by its feet. But they weren't really feet now he looked, more like bone hooves – thin and almost pointed.

'This ends here, boy,' said the figure. 'You have delayed our crossing long enough. It is only because you are related to this human who will bring us into your world that you are still alive. But even that will not save you if you continue to stand in our way.'

When the armoured shadow spoke there was no movement of its head or mouth. The sound seemed to come from all around, as if the mist was speaking for him. Its voice was commanding and deep but not menacing. It was almost hypnotic. Alexander found that he was lost for words. Swaying stupidly he tried to think what to do but the magnitude of the situation threatened to drown him.

'You can't – I can't let you,' Alexander stammered weakly.

'You say that as if you have a choice,' the shadow lord replied.

'You're killing people from our world. Innocent people. Children. Your world has to stop.'

'You think of our world and your world as if they are different things. That is too simplistic a view, child. Our worlds are inextricably linked. We are the different halves of the same world. Conjoined twins. What happens in your world has consequences in ours. A tree falls in your world and a storm rages in ours. A king dies in our world, and a town is flooded or a volcano erupts or a plague is spread in yours. Our worlds were once almost identical, but as your world flourished ours began to die. We have paid the price so that you humans may live as you do.' Its voice grew more intense and it stepped a little closer. 'Now your father will set us free. He knew you would come. We have been watching you since you arrived.'

'Why? Why do you want to come? Why can't you just stay where you are?'

'The creatures you have seen here are mere insects. There are beings on our side of the world that stretch across the entire sky. Creatures that wake from underground and crawl over our villages like they were only pebbles and we dare not venture onto the seas. They have been lost to us for thousands of years. All we need is an oasis in your world – a place of refuge that my people can escape to. You can join your father by our side. Help us reclaim this village, repair the work that you have sabotaged, become a pioneer of a new beginning for both our worlds.' He turned and strode a few paces away, gazing back into his own world. 'Or don't, and we shall be forced to use your body to unlock another portal. You'll be stranded. Stuck between worlds for eternity. Your frozen life-force merely a tool to keep the gateway open. Not dead but not truly alive.'

Alexander looked to his father, who smiled at him and nodded. For a moment, time seemed to freeze and he was washed with a calming clarity as if his mind had suddenly thawed from a long stasis. He could think freely, deeply, logically as the Professor had taught him.

'How many are there in your species?'

'There are many tribes,' the shadow replied.

'You're never just going to just stop at this village are you?' he asked, his fingers feeling out the strings of his violin still in his hand.

His father began to walk towards him, and Alexander raised the violin to his shoulder.

'I'm warning you. Don't do anything stupid,' his father said.

'I'm afraid you lost your right to tell me what to do a long time ago!' Alexander said placing the bow over the strings.

'You go to play a single note on that thing and you will force me to take action,' his father said, his face flushing as he took another step closer. The shadow walked back into the room from the edge of the other world, sensing the danger in Alexander's hands. The shadow, hidden deep in that shell of bone, seemed to tense, coil like a cat ready to attack. Alexander slowly nodded, his eyes downcast and lowered his hand, his bow tumbling to the floor. His right hand sank into his pocket and he dropped his head submissively.

'Good boy,' his father said. 'Good boy.'

Alexander pulled his hand out of his pocket and threw the compound into his father's face. His father cried out, grabbing at his burning eyes and dropping to his knees.

'No!' the shadow lord cried out, grabbing his father with one hand and carrying him off as if he were a doll. The creature ran through the portal and off into the mist of the other world before Alexander had even managed to grab his bow from the floor and close the gateway. They had escaped.

Just then, the door burst open and a crowd of villagers led by Arty, Nathan and Lucy came tumbling in. They looked to Alexander, then straight to the portal and the frozen bodies of the villagers, and they stared open mouthed.

'Alex, are you okay?' the Professor said, leaning heavily on

Nathan for support as he hobbled inside the study. Alexander nodded, the violin still resting on his shoulder. 'You need to shut this portal and release the last of the villagers.'

'Then it's over?' Arty asked.

'No,' Alexander replied without a pause and everyone turned to look. 'I can't shut the portal – not properly. I'll free the villagers now, but we still need to save Edgar, Lord Bleakhope's son. We came here to save the villagers. All of them. That includes him. This all began with him and it will only truly finish when he returns. He's still in that other world and I'm going to get him. Besides, if anything from our world remains in that other realm, then we won't have restored the balance. Things will still be able to cross back. I have to go in there and find Edgar. I'm going into the other realm.'

10

The Edge

'WE DON'T EVEN KNOW IF EDGAR is actually in that world. And if he is, I doubt he is still alive, Alex,' the Professor said, not as matter-of-factly as he normally sounded. It was softened with what might have been sympathy or maybe even admiration.

'No, my father said he had seen him. If there's a chance he is still alive we must try to get him back.' The Professor stood looking at him for a while. Possibly he was redefining Alexander in a new light, but far more likely, Alexander thought, was that he was calculating all possible scenarios.

'If we all travel through, that would mean upsetting the balance between our worlds even further. More creatures from their world will be able to pass back. We have just spent the last few days trying to stop that. And I will be of no use to you,' he said, looking down at his bandaged leg.

'Then I'll go alone.'

'No you won't!' Arty said sternly. 'I'm coming with you.'

Lucy stepped in front of her father. 'Me too.'

'Lucy, I've just got you back. I'm not going to let – ' Old Dan said, putting his hand protectively on his daughter's shoulder.

'Father, I have to. I can't carry on living like before, knowing I didn't try to help someone else trapped there like I was. Besides, apart from you and uncle, I'm the best tracker in the whole county. Alex will need me!'

Old Dan went to say something else, but slowly closed his mouth and nodded.

'Three is a lot of people going through still. It will mean that something big could cross back. We will need people to stay here and fend off whatever comes through,' the Professor said, ending with a wince and grabbing his leg.

'I'll stick around,' Nathan said, leaning on his pitchfork.

'Time seems to be different in their world. We could be gone days but it will only be hours for us, so don't give up hope,' Alexander said, looking around him at the faces of the villagers. He was safe. There was fading blue sky outside the window, and sunlight shining into the study windows. He could walk away from this and know he had done his best. He could tell himself he didn't have to do it. But he knew his father's mistakes had to be undone.

Placing the violin on his shoulder again, he played a low G. The villagers being used as keys appeared solid and alive and the portal shrank to a thin slither but, unlike before, it never disappeared. There was a brief respite as villagers grabbed and hugged loved ones as they began to wake up and Alexander used the time to stuff his pockets full of possibly useful items – a compass, some string, a box of matches and a penknife. Many of the villagers wished him luck before taking the weak and wounded back to the tavern. Just Old Dan, Nathan and the Professor remained now.

Alexander took a deep breath. Walking towards the tear between their worlds, he stopped at the edge – the edge of his world and this other. Lucy and Arty came and stood next to him. He could feel the cold drifting in from the other realm, the mist spilling down around him, leaking in from the other side. After looking behind him once more to the Professor he smiled, turned back to the portal and took a step. A small step to cover a huge distance.

In the dark, new world in which they found themselves the air was thick with damp and cold and it carried on it a sickly smell of decay and mould. The trees around him were the ones Alexander had seen before, standing on giant roots like stilts out of the mist and stretching off into the grey gloom above them like dark pillars holding up a grey sky. Deep, bird-like noises echoed through the roots.

'We should get moving,' Arty said, gazing around. 'Any idea where? He could be anywhere?'

Alexander took the compass out of his pocket. The needle slowly swung around in circles never stopping. 'Well, this isn't going to be any help,' he said, putting it back into his pocket.

'Look!' Lucy said, pointing to a patch of mud a few feet away. She walked over and knelt down beside the mud. 'Footprints. Small too.'

'Where do they lead?' Alexander asked, crouching next to her. Lucy didn't answer. She stood up and followed the tracks off below one of the massive trees. The others paced slowly behind her as she carefully made her way down a shallow slope, stooping over to see the footprints.

The tracks, which Alexander had a hard time picking out, seemed to be easy for Lucy to follow. The footprints led under the first few trees, a good ten minute walk, and stopped as the mud turned to jet-black rock that rose up into sharp spires like a of forest of rotten dragon teeth.

'What do we do now?' Arty asked. 'The tracks stop here.'

'No, they don't,' Lucy said, kneeling down again and squinting at something on the rocks. 'There are some scuff marks here.' Alexander leaned in but couldn't see anything. 'And here, look! Some strands of wool where he must have brushed his arm.'

'How did you even notice that?' Alexander asked, struggling to see the fibres even now that they had been pointed out to him.

'Father and my uncle. They used to track poachers and the like. You couldn't help but pick some bits up,' she said with a smile.

'I'm glad you came along,' Alexander said, and felt himself turning red immediately after he had said it.

Trekking through the rock spires was slow work and it made Alexander nervous. Noises came from all around in the mist that blanketed everything. They had been in the other world for hours now and he just wanted to get moving. But Lucy would walk a few yards in one direction then return and lead off in another, trying to pick up the almost invisible trail.

'I think we're getting close,' Lucy said, looking around her as what little light there was started to fade.

Alexander moved up next to her. 'How can you tell?'

'The tracks have been getting more regular, as if he has been moving around here a lot. Backwards and forwards.'

She continued to move between the stone stalagmites with growing confidence until they came to a place where the rock spires had collapsed into a heap. Perhaps they had toppled under their own weight Alexander hoped, but there were worrying signs that they had been knocked down by something monstrously huge. The fallen towers of rock had formed impassable mounds of rubble with nooks and holes that they had to squeeze through. They had only begun to make their way over and under the stones when they found Edgar.

His eyes were wide and fearful, his arms wrapped around his knees, pushed as far back into his little cave as he could go. The whites of his eyes seemed to glow and the skin around his face was smeared with mud. His hair was long and jagged and streaked with dirt. He still wore some of what must have been his original clothes, long socks, shorts and a shirt, but they were torn and covered in grime. Around his bare and bruised feet lay the skins of some strange, dark green fruit. Arty leant over to reach for him and the boy snapped out, biting Arty and then curling back up and hissing like a trapped reptile.

'Ow!' Arty yelled and shook his bitten hand. Lucy pushed Arty out of the way and knelt down at the entrance to the hole.

'Hey, it's Edgar, isn't it? I remember you from the manor house. My name's Lucy. I come from the village. Do you remember me?' Lucy said in such a sweet and melodic voice that the boy stopped hissing almost immediately. He stared at her for a long while. 'We're here to help you, Edgar. We're here to get you home. Do you want to go home?'

Edgar looked back at her for a long while without blinking, then nodded almost imperceptibly.

'That's great. Do you want to hold my hand?' Lucy asked, and very slowly edged her hand towards him, stopping just in front of his feet.

There was a tense pause before he began to relax one arm from the iron grip it had around his knees and stretched out to meet hers. Lucy gripped his hand and the boy began to sob. He didn't resist as she pulled him out of the hole and drew him into a hug. Wrapping his arms around her, he buried his face into her neck.

The moment was cut short by the alien roar of some far off beast. Edgar jumped and tried to wriggle free from Lucy's arms and scramble back into his hole.

'You're safe. You're safe. We're getting out of here!' she said, keeping a tight grip on his waist and making shushing sounds.

'Agreed. Let's get out of here!' Alexander said, and began to lead the way back through the maze of rocks. It proved almost impossible at once though. Hurrying as they were, they had lost sight of the trail that had led them there. The pillars of rock looked identical and with no horizon there was no way to judge their direction.

A screech above made Alexander look up and go crashing into a rock that was jutting out of the ground. Blood immediately began to run down the side of his face. Alexander hardly noticed though as he stared up at the massive silhouette of a winged creature circling above them in the low hanging clouds. Edgar tore himself free from Lucy's arms but instead of running back, he ran up to where Alexander had fallen. He scooped up a handful of mud and pressed it to Alexander's head where he had cut himself. After he had done this he seemed to relax a little.

'Blood,' Edgar said so quietly it was almost a whisper. 'They can smell it.' Alexander went to touch his head but Edgar pulled his arm away.

'Thank you,' Alexander answered.

'We should keep moving!' Arty said, grabbing Alexander's arm and pulling him up.

'But where? Which direction?' Alexander asked, petrified of the thing above them.

'Hey, look,' Lucy said, pointing to Edgar who in turn was pointing off between two rock towers. 'Is that the way back to the portal – the way back to our world?' Edgar nodded and lowered his hand. Arty went to pick the boy up but Edgar shook his head and ran to Lucy. 'Arty looks ugly, but he's okay,' Lucy explained to Edgar with a smile.

'Thanks,' Arty said, looking offended, although Alexander suspected he was just playing along.

They followed Edgar's directions until they reached the edge of the rocky maze and came back to the forest of monolithic trees. Once they were underneath the first giant tree they felt a little safer now that they were out of sight of whatever it was that had circled above.

'Not far now,' Alexander said, more to himself to calm his racing heart than the others but they still nodded. That was when they saw the shadow drift in front of them. It was not like the shadows that had chased Alexander when he first arrived at the village and into the pond. This shadow was formless and shapeless, like a dark cloud of smoke that glided along the ground. It moved, not towards them but across their path to a pile of dry sticks that looked worryingly like the beginnings of a giant nest. For a moment, the shadow just hovered above the pile, then it sank into the middle of the sticks. The four of them just stood and stared, waiting for something to happen. Then the darkness wrapped itself around the twigs like fast growing ivy and pulled them up around itself. More and more twigs were pulled towards it, moulded and bent to take on a shape. Suddenly it was clear what form it was taking – that of a man. Like the moving scarecrows Alexander had seen before, the darkness had made itself a body of sticks. Its face was featureless, just an elongated head. Its body made of tightly woven branches, its hands long, thin twigs. For a moment there was no sound but their heavy breathing as they stood rooted to the spot watching in awe as the stickman took shape. Then it suddenly moved, lurching towards them. Alexander screamed and Lucy grabbed him and Edgar and pulled them away. They ran out from under the tree and towards the next one, the stickman moving jerkily after them. Sprinting on they opened up a small gap between them and their pursuer.

'There it is!' Lucy cried, and they could all see it now – the portal and their doorway home. It was a bright sliver of light

from the edge of their world in the distance, burning through
the fog of that dark land like a lighthouse to guide them home.
They were close, less than a hundred yards or so away, and
Alexander even allowed himself to think they were going to make
it, when his father and the shadow lord stepped in front of them,
blocking their way.

11

The End

'IT ENDS HERE, ALEXANDER,' HIS FATHER said, as the four of them came to a skidding halt in front of the shadow lord. 'Come with us. Let me show you this world and its treasures and wonders. Let us be part of something great together.'

'I'm not leaving my friends,' Alexander said, stepping in front of Lucy and Edgar, the shock, fear and awe from their first meeting having melted away.

'He has made his choice,' the shadow lord said. 'I will put them all into suspension. Keys for you to use.'

'Wait, he'll see reason,' Alexander's father said, now stepping in front of the armoured shadow. 'I just need more time. I just need – '

'No!' the shadow growled and the ground shuddered. 'My masters grow impatient. If your son will not come with you, then he will serve us in a different way.' The shadow finished, pushing Alexander's father out of the way as if he were a small boy at his feet. He stepped forward and towered over Alexander reaching out towards his heart with a huge hand of intense darkness. Arty charged towards the shadow with a roar, hammer held high. The shadow swatted at him and Arty was knocked flying. Alexander stepped back, his arms out to try to protect Lucy and Edgar who were still behind him. The shadow hand continued to reach towards Alexander's heart and cold washed over him. It was as if the shadow's proximity was opening up a hole in his chest where his own warmth was spilling out to be replaced with ice.

'No!' his father cried, and shoved Alexander out of the way. The shadow angrily swung its gaze to his father and then buried its hand into his father's chest with a brutal lunge. His father gasped for air – his eyes wild with shock and then he collapsed to the floor translucent and shadowy. Alexander stared at the scene in shock.

'Come on!' Lucy cried, dragging Edgar behind her and running towards the portal. The shadow lord cried out in rage.

'Look what you have made me do!' It strode towards Alexander with giant steps.

'Arty, get my father!' Alexander shouted, retreating back towards the giant tree. Arty ran over to his father and seemed to be able to pick him up as if he was hardly there. Not wanting to lose sight of the portal, Alexander tried to circle around behind his pursuer, but the shadow lord was just too tall and quick. It did not seem to care about the others escaping behind him. He was focused solely on Alexander now. That should have terrified him, but he was glad. If he were to die here, at least he would have saved the others. He wasn't planning on dying though. He desperately searched his pockets for a weapon or tool. There was the compass, a penknife and the box of matches. He doubted the penknife would do much damage and the compass had proven to be useless. He would have to run, he decided. Run and hide and try to survive like Edgar had done until he could find a safe time to return, but as he turned to flee back towards the direction of the rock forest, the stickman came shambling towards him. Alexander froze, trapped between the wickerman and the shadow lord.

'As long as you remain here the way between our worlds will stay open. The loss of your father will delay us, but we will discover the secrets he has hidden from us in good time.'

The stickman was just a few yards away now and he felt its thorny hand reach up to grab his shoulder. Alexander spun around and lit the match he now held in his hand, dropping it back into the matchbox. With the box held in his fist, he punched a hole in the stickman's chest and let go. The other matches flared to life – the potassium chlorate and sulphur igniting in a bright white glow. The stickman stumbled back as the fire inside it took hold, setting the small twigs ablaze. Alexander grabbed the wickerman's arm as it began to topple and swung it towards the shadow lord. The darkness that had possessed the sticks seemed to give the flames fuel and explode, setting the whole thing up into a roaring column of fire. The blazing wickerman crashed into the shadow lord, who let out a howl and fell back in a shower of sparks.

Alexander did not wait. He sprinted past them towards the portal, clutching his bleeding hand. His knuckles, where he had punched the stickman, throbbed but his adrenaline kept the pain at bay. He risked a glance back and saw the shadow lord pushing the flaming wreckage off himself and getting to his hooves. The mist and giant tree roots passed in a blur as Alexander pelted on closer and closer to home. He could hear the shadow gaining fast, its long strides now just behind him.

Through the portal he saw the Professor was waiting for him, beckoning him on until Alexander was there bursting through the portal. Alexander raced into the waiting arms of the Professor who grabbed him as he crashed into a panting heap. Alexander turned to see the shadow lord on the edge of their world, standing on the other side of the portal.

'Play!' the Professor said, pushing Alexander to his feet, his leg seemingly healed. Alexander took the violin that the Professor grabbed from the table. His right hand was swollen and ached, but he could still play.

'Nooo!' the shadow lord cried out from the other world as Alexander put the violin to his shoulder and positioned his fingers. He drew the bow slowly across the strings and the deep, resonating note rang out. A cloud of compound rose from the Professor's hand and vibrated instantly making the whole world shimmer. Nathan and the Professor covered their ears as the note seemed to intensify but Alexander played on, the note almost deafening him. Falling to his knees, the shadow lord cried something out that was in no language Alexander could understand. Then, with a loud crack, the other world vanished. Not a sliver of the portal remained.

The violin note was still ringing in his ears and echoed about the room as the Professor walked over to Alexander and hugged him. Not a manly pat on the back or quick tap on the shoulder – a hug. It was such an unexpected act that Alexander just stood there for a moment before he squeezed him back.

'Well done,' Professor Cordite said, smiling down at him.

'Thank you,' Alexander beamed, stepping back. 'Where are the others? Are they alright?' Alexander asked. 'Where is my father?'

'Do not worry. They came back through the portal many hours ago. Lucy has taken Edgar to see his father. In the weeks since you passed into that other world he has recovered well. Arty came through a few hours after Lucy, carrying your father. Your father is now recovering at the tavern. His form seemed to return when he crossed over, although his recovery is taking far longer than the others. He is being constantly watched by Arty and will be returning with us to Cambridge.'

'What will happen to him now?' Alexander asked.

'Well, I can hardly take him to the magistrate, can I? I would be laughed out of court if I tried to explain he was guilty of opening a dimensional portal. He will have to remain our guest until I can figure out what to do with him.'

'So it's over now? For good?' Alexander asked, and the Professor nodded.

'It is.'

When Alexander woke the next morning it was with the sun streaming onto his face through the thin curtains. He swung his legs over the bed and stood up, stretching. He walked over, flung open the curtains, unhooked the latches and pushed at the windows. They swung open and a sweet summer breeze wafted in. Blue skies stretched overhead in all directions and he stood there for a moment with a silly grin on his face and let himself be warmed by the sun. The fields and grass all around had returned to vibrant greens and golds, and he almost laughed when a flock of starlings flew overhead towards the orchard. When he turned back to the room, his heart sank a little as he saw his packed-up belongings.

In no hurry to leave, he dressed slowly, slung his violin over his shoulder and picked up the large trunk. He dragged the trunk out into the corridor and started to bump it down the stairs. There, at the bottom, everyone was waiting for him. The Professor stood by his bags looking at his pocket watch. Nathan ran up the stairs to meet him and picked up the trunk with one hand and carried it down for him. Lucy pushed through the crowd to greet him first.

They stared at each other for a while. Alexander thought of a thousand things to say but none of them were right.

'Will you come back?' Lucy asked, sounding calm and collected, but Alexander saw her bottom lip quiver slightly.

'I hope so. The Professor is keen to return to Cambridge to check his correspondence and find somewhere my father can go so that he is no longer a threat. But he was saying that the veil is still thin here, even if there are no open portals. It might be a good place to carry out some experiments and set up base for a while.' She smiled at this.

'Alexander, you can't leave us without another song!' Mr Parnell said, stepping forward and holding him firmly by the shoulders. Alexander looked at the Professor who checked his pocket watch and then nodded to him with a smile. Alexander unlatched his case and took out his violin with his bandaged hand.

'Of course. Just one more song.'

Acknowledgements

A huge thank you to Peter Randall, Janet Davidson, Patrick Ramsey, and James Hodgson from Greenwich Exchange Publishing. Thanks, as always, to my wife for her undying support and promotion – and to my two boys who sometimes let me tap out a few words every now and then.

ALSO BY
STUART FRYD
from GREENWICH
EXCHANGE

THE LOST AND DROWNED

ISBN: 978-1-910996-11-9 128 pages

Every winter girls are going missing.

Lydia and her carefree sister Sophie must stay alive long enough to uncover the terrible, supernatural force that stalks the children of Rottenhall Orphanage.

With the help of some strange, magical gifts can Lydia defy the odds, survive the dangers of Regency London and overcome her nightmarish adversary?

Download (PDF Format, 620K) Free Teaching Resources for *The Lost and Drowned* including: Guided Reading activities, Writing tasks and Grammar activities all designed for KS2 SATs revision.

Stuart Fryd is a father, a husband, a reader and a dreamer. Occasionally, as was the case with this book, he writes those dreams down, if only to stop him thinking about them when he really should be concentrating on other things. You can follow him on Twitter@Stuartfryd. Also go over to www.thelostanddrowned.com for more news, videos, lesson plans and information about the book and author.